My Uncle Makes Dolls to Replace Souls in Hell

Brandon Faircloth

Other Works by Brandon Faircloth:

Mystery

Darkness

On the Hill and Other Tales of Horror

Whimsical Leprosy

The Outsiders: Book One

You saw something you shouldn't have

One Bite at a Time

The Outsiders: Book Two (*Coming Soon*)

Table of Contents

My uncle makes dolls to replace souls in hell.

<u>Part One</u>

Hell is a forest deep and dark.

Its earth is cold, its trees are stark.

Among the shades dwells the Hunter's face,

please send another in my place.

My Uncle Teddy gave me a book of Old World fairy tales when I was little. It was filled with stories full of blood and terror far different than the modern versions you see today. But there was this poem at the end of the book that was different than the rest, and that was the thing that always stuck with me, always spooked me even when I got older.

I thought of it again when I was sitting at my uncle's wake three weeks ago. Staring at strangers milling around the casket and funeral sprays, my eyes landed on a photo display that had been set up showing various pictures of my Uncle from a little boy on up to his mid-fifties when he died. It reminded me that I didn't really know him very well.

He only visited a couple of times when I was 8 or 9, and while I know he called and checked in with my father periodically, my main sense of the man was a vague impression from stories of my father's childhood and that book of fairy tales. I suppressed a small shiver. Was that poem part of the book or written in? I couldn't remember now. And what kind of man was my…

"He is a wonderful man, isn't he, Dilly?"

I snapped out of my reverie to see two old women standing stoop-shouldered and solemn just a few feet away. They reminded me of a pair of wizened buzzards tucking into a good meal, except I supposed funeral stalking old women fed more on despair than spoiled meat. Chiding myself for the unkind thought, I offered a weak smile as I saw they were looking at me.

"Oh yes, a truly singular man of truly singular talents, Milly," the other one offered, her eyes not leaving my face.

Swallowing, I accepted they weren't going to just go away, and so I decided to engage them in the hopes of getting it over quickly. "So you two knew my Uncle well?"

Milly gave a low throaty chuckle that spoke of cigarettes and bourbon earlier in life if not now. "Oh yes. Fairly well. We've been clients of his for years."

I felt a small flicker of interest at that. "Clients? You know, I always wondered what my Uncle Teddy did. He always had a lot of money from what I heard, but I never knew from what. Can you tell me what kind of work he did?"

The two women exchanged a glance and then a giggle. It was a short, nasty sound like schoolgirls sharing the secret of the cat they had just lit on fire. I felt myself recoil slightly and was about to make an excuse and go when Dilly started speaking again.

"He is an artist, my dear. Painfully talented. The thing we use him for are our memoriam dolls. I have one made every year." She said this last with some amount of pride or boasting in her voice, but I had no idea what she was talking about. Whatever it was, it clearly rankled Milly, whose mouth drew down into a sullen frown.

"Not everyone got all of their father's and husband's fortunes, Dilly. And besides, Theodore always said that once every five years was quite sufficient. "

Dilly sniffed, her painted on eyebrows arching slightly. "Well, time will tell, I suppose. I prefer to have the least amount of time in the woods as possible."

I froze. "The woods? What woods?"

Dilly looked at Milly again before giving me a sly smile. "Oh, nothing for a sweet, young girl like you to worry about, I'm sure."

Milly leaned forward and touched my forearm, sending a crawl of flesh up to my neck as I stepped back. "We just wanted to come by and tell you what a remarkable man your uncle is. Good to meet you." And then the pair were gone back into the crowd.

Is, not was. She kept saying is. It could have been a simple mistake, of course, but it didn't feel like that. Not from those two at least, and not over and over. As I looked around, I realized I was getting a similar, unsettling vibe from many of the people that were there. A lot of them were older, and almost all of them were wealthy-looking. But that wasn't what bothered me. They all seemed to know each other and they all kept looking at me. I hadn't noticed earlier, but now I could see the furtive glances, the shared looks, the sense that everyone else in the room was in on some joke that I didn't even know had been told.

I wanted to pay my respects to my uncle, and I was the only family member left to do it, but fuck this. I left the funeral home and got in my rental car. It was too late to get a flight that night, but my plan was to be gone by the next morning.

****

I woke up slapping at my phone, momentarily

disoriented by the strange surroundings of my hotel room. At first I thought it was my alarm, but then I realized it was a phone call. I didn't recognize the number and almost didn't answer at all, but when I did, I heard the rolling Southern accent of an older man. He identified himself as Hershel Myers, my uncle's attorney. He needed to meet with me before I left town on matters dealing with my uncle's estate.

On the drive to the lawyer's office, I admit to feeling some level of excitement that I might be about to get a large random inheritance from the cliché rich dead uncle I barely knew. I didn't know Teddy well enough to feel guilty for not mourning him more, and I could certainly use the money. But sitting across the desk from Myers, I felt a growing unease. It sounded stupid even as I thought it, but he somehow reminded me of those creepy old women from the night before.

He was talking to me with an oily cheerfulness, his ruddy cheeks perched above swaying jowls that hung like meat in a butcher shop window. He was making small talk at first, talking about how great a man my uncle is — again, is, not was — and how he had counted Uncle Teddy as a dear friend for decades. Blah, blah, Mr. Creepy. Show me the money so I can go take a shower.

And there was money to be had, with certain conditions. If I followed those conditions perfectly, I would receive a cashier's check for $500,000.00. As it fell under inheritance, there weren't even any taxes to be paid on it. I asked what I had to do and how fast I could do it, and Mr. Creepy grinned.

"I like your spunk, girl. You remind me of Theodore more than a little." He stood up and went to a large table against one wall of the sprawling office. Picking up a polished wooden box from the table, he brought it over to sit before me on the desk. The wood was of a deep gray with whorls of wood grain tracing their way around a large silver lock that secured the front of the box. Myers handed me a small envelope and I could feel the heft of one or more small keys inside.

"It works like this. Inside this envelope is a key to this box, a key to your uncle's home and instructions. You go to his home tonight, and follow those instructions at precisely 9 p.m. Not before or after. If you do that, tomorrow morning you will come back here and receive your check for $500,000.00. How does that sound?"

I smiled, my hand greasy on the envelope. "That sounds just fine."

****

Hello, Cora. You don't know me well, but my hope is that you will indulge me in this thing I ask, as you are the only one I can ask. I understand you'll find this all very strange, but please do it as precisely as you can. Tonight, go to my house. You will find a door on the right side of the front hall that leads to a large empty room with a pattern in the marble of the floor. You will find a small table in the corner containing twelve small branches, a small bottle of lighter fluid, a knife and a box of matches.

Arrange the branches where two of them are side-by-side and point in each of the four cardinal directions: North, South, East and West. For guidance, the fireplace in the room is precisely North. Set the other four branches between the outer edge of the cardinal branches so that each branch connects two sets of two.

Set the doll you find in the box in the middle of the branches. Take the knife and prick your finger. Press the blood to the doll's face. A drop or two will do fine. Douse the doll and the branches in lighter fluid and light it with a match. After it is burning, leave the house immediately and return to Mr. Myers' office the following morning for your reward.

Thank you for helping me Cora. I wish we had been closer. Perhaps someday we will be.

****

The box did contain a doll, though it was unlike anything I had ever seen before. It was a remarkable likeness of my Uncle Teddy, with a face carved out of ivory and a body made from the same strange gray wood as the box that held it. In the middle of the thing's chest was a small compartment made of smoked glass about the size of a dime. I saw no way to open the glass, but inside it I could see what looked like a small tuft of hair.

For the tenth time since opening the box, I debated just leaving. My uncle's house was very nice, and the room where I was supposed to burn the doll was actually kind of beautiful, but the idea of doing some bizarre ritual with the weird doll was sending up all kinds of warning signals. I had gotten to the house a bit early and checked it out, and as far as I could tell, no one else was there and there were no signs of cameras. How would the lawyer even know if I did the dumb ritual?

Still, did I really want to risk $500,000.00? And it's not like I'm superstitious. So what if my rich uncle was eccentric? If his dying wish was to have his creepy effigy burned, who was it hurting?

Fuck it. It was 8:58, and I was behind schedule.

The branches were easy, but the blood was a bit harder. I'm a little squeamish, particularly when it comes to intentionally cutting myself. But I got it done. The tip of the knife was sharp, so a quick poke of my thumb and a thick bead of dark blood welled up almost instantly. Pressing my thumb to the face of the doll, I thought I felt it give under the light pressure I applied, almost as though its surface was made of thin rubber instead of carved ivory.

I pulled my finger away quickly and saw the smear of blood on the creamy surface of Teddy's face, but then it was gone. It had been absorbed into the doll, which seemed several pounds heavier now. I had to grab it with my bloody hand to keep hold of it, and after fumbling for a moment I sat it down in the middle of the branches I had arranged.

Lighter fluid. Fire. Doll in flames.

And I was going to leave. I should have left. My job was done, and the instructions said for me to leave the house as soon as I got done setting the fire. But I didn't.

At first, I told myself I was making sure that the fire didn't go out too quickly. That I was ensuring that it was a job completed and well done. But that wasn't the real reason, or at least not the most compelling one.

I wanted to stay in case something actually happened.

The doll burned slowly at first, but after a couple of minutes the wood of its body began to glow orange with the heat of the flames. The smoke coming up from the doll was a strange green and seemed thicker than it should have been, almost like a liquid being poured up into the ceiling. Then there was a cracking sound and a flash of light.

The doll was gone and my uncle was sitting there, naked and bleeding from a claw wound across his chest. He looked around the room, his expression blossoming with relief as he took it in. Shifting to the balls of his feet, he looked at his left hand, which appeared to be full of some kind of black, wiry hair. Then he looked back up, directly at me.

"Hi there, Cora. You were supposed to already be gone."

I swallowed and took a step back. "Um, sorry. I can go now."

He shook his head as he stood up, his expression hard and his eyes unreadable. "I don't think so. It's too late for that. We need to talk."

Part Two

"So you didn't die."

We were sitting in a large, comfortable parlor on the other side of the hall from where I had burned the doll a few minutes earlier. After forbidding me to leave, Teddy had carefully placed the black hair he held in a small glass jar tucked away in the shadows of a recessed wall shelf. Only then did he step out of the room briefly to retrieve a crimson robe. Beckoning me to follow, he led me across to where we currently sat, his hands clasped in his lap as he regarded me with a small smile.

"No, I did. What did they tell you killed me?"

I started slightly at that, but decided to go along with it for now. I didn't believe he had been dead, of course, but I knew something was going on, and while I couldn't rule out an elaborate trick of some kind, it seemed unlikely. "Okay, um. They said it was a stroke."

He winced. "Shit. I'll have to watch out for that. I need to eat healthier for one thing." His smile widened. "But I'm getting off-topic. You saw something pretty remarkable tonight I guess. And you deserve an explanation."

Nodding, I shifted in my chair. "Yeah, that'd be nice. I'm kind of freaked out right now. And please be honest. I know you faked your death."

Teddy raised an eyebrow. "Faked my death? No, I was really dead. They really buried my body. In fact, that body is still laying there rotting as we speak."

"But how? That makes no sense. How are you here then?"

He leaned forward, his eyes glittering in the meager light offered by the lamps set in the distant corners of the room. "Because I went to Hell and you brought me back."

I stood up. "Look, I don't have time for this weird bullshit. Pay me my money and I'll be out of your hair."

He waved his hand, gesturing for me to sit back down. "Calm down. You need to hear me out, believe me. For your own good."

I sunk down into the chair again, a ball of ice slowly forming in my stomach. "Why? Why for my own good?"

Teddy sighed. "Look, I didn't want to involve you in this. You're Sam's kid, and you always seemed like a sweet girl. But you're the only blood kin I have left, and it has to be blood kin for the ritual to work. If you had left like you were supposed to, no harm, no foul. But you didn't."

I frowned, my stomach twisting further. "So? I can just leave now."

He shook his head. "You can, but I wouldn't. Not yet." Teddy raised a finger. "Let me explain. Describe to me the people that were at my wake. Better yet, let me tell you. A bunch of well-heeled, slightly creepy strangers, right? Maybe overly friendly to you for no apparent reason?"

Nodding, I swallowed before answering. "Yeah. They were really weird. Especially Dilly and Milly."

My uncle's eyes widened slightly. "Shit, I should have guessed. Stay away from them. They are very dangerous." He ran his hand through his hair. "Fuck, they're all very dangerous. But the point is this. My death, and my return, are of utmost importance to these people. There are probably half a dozen people watching this house right now, and some of them will already know that I'm back and you haven't left yet. Which means you might be learning things they want kept secret."

"Ok. Like what?"

Sitting back, his expression dark, Uncle Teddy began to explain.

****

When I was in my twenties, I came out here to try and make a living as an artist. As you might expect, that went about as well for me as it does for most. Within six weeks I was close to starving, and no one had bought a single one of my paintings or sculptures. I was on the verge on selling my remaining art supplies and using the money to buy a bus ticket back home.

Then one day I was sitting in a park whittling when a well-dressed man approached me and sat down. At first he just watched me carving. I was making a small face out of an irregular piece of wood I had found in an alley the day before. Back then I was in the habit of looking down alleyways for cans and bottles to turn in for change, but I also would sometimes run across a piece of wood I could work on for a bit. I never thought to try to sell my carvings, but it calmed my nerves.

Still, this man was intently watching me work. It was strange, but I ignored it and focused on my carving. After a few more minutes he spoke, telling me how talented I was. Had I been carving for long? Had I ever made toys or dolls?

I was getting some alarm bells — even just a few weeks in this city and I had shed most of my small town naivete. I felt like this was leading to some kind of sexual come on, but I was wrong. The man said he was part of a group that was looking for an artist to make some dolls to very specific specifications, and would I be interested. He then threw in that it paid very well.

It was an easy decision. I accepted immediately and tried to ask some questions to give the illusion that I knew what I was talking about and that he had just hired a professional. The fact that he had approached me because I looked so desperate didn't occur to me until some time later.

He told me that he would bring me a book that explained everything I'd need to know about the construction of the dolls, as well as "the materials" I would need. He asked if I read Latin or French, and when I looked at him apprehensively, he waved the question away, saying to nevermind, the illustrations should suffice.

Two days later I was in my shitty apartment surrounded by recent deliveries of wood and ivory, along with a small rotary saw and set of dental drills for carving the ivory. I was sitting on the floor, a large leather-bound book spread across my lap, my hands gripping its edges tightly.

I didn't read Latin or French, but my employer had been right. The illustrations sufficed. This was some kind of occult book, detailing a variety of depraved acts and rituals, and while I couldn't be sure, it seemed that there was more than one involving the summoning and controlling of spirits or demons. This frightened me, but then I reached the pages involving the "*poupees memoriam*", which I learned was French for "memoriam dolls".

The basic construction of the dolls was fairly simple. Wood body, with joints at the shoulders and hips. Ivory head, carved in the distinct likeness of the person to be bound to the doll. A recess in the body of the doll containing the hair or flesh of that same person. Oh, I've improved on the design over the years, but only aesthetically. You'd be surprised how competitive these people get over how their dolls look or who has the fanciest one.

Still, back then, I was terrified both of the people I had gotten involved with and what would happen if I failed to get the job done. I could have just left town then, and I wish now that I had. But back then I was young and stupid, and I didn't want to go home a failure. I was supposed to get $5,000.00 for completing the doll, and as you might know, that was a great deal of money thirty years ago. So I set to work.

The first time I made a memoriam doll, it took me nearly a month. I kept restarting, you see. I went through half the materials I was given before I finally decided I needed to take a step back and quit overthinking it. Give myself over to it. When I started back, it was entirely different. I just carved, and the shapes flowed out. In eight hours I was done, and it was far better than anything I had ever done. When I held that finished doll, it was like I was looking into the heart of my mysterious benefactor. I had made something true. Something powerful and real. And that's what really hooked me.

I believe everyone has some thing or things they are meant to do. They're built for it, destined for it, call it what you like. But when you find your thing, you know it. And I had found mine.

Mr. Darrow, as he introduced himself after seeing the doll, was ecstatic at my handiwork. He studied it closely, turning it this way and that. He glanced up at me a couple of times, asking how I knew to carve this line or that curve into the doll's rigid flesh. Lines that weren't in the book's illustrations. I shrugged, no longer nervous. I just knew that they were supposed to be there, I replied.

The man nodded, his eyes growing damp as he completed his examination of the doll. "It's beautiful. It's perfect." He suddenly reached forward and gave me an awkward hug. "Thank you so much. Thank you thank you thank you." He regained some of his self-control and stepped back, wiping his eyes. "You are about to become a very wealthy young man."

And he was right. Darrow was part of a massive

network of the rich and powerful that wanted their own dolls. And they were paying $500k a doll now, then later a million. Within five years I had enough that I never had to worry about money again. But it never occurred to me to stop making the dolls. I loved the work, and they wouldn't have let me anyway.

These people…they are very bad people. I always knew from the first time looking at that book that I was dealing with something supernatural. At first, I figured it was some kind of voodoo or something. Then I thought it was some bored rich fucks that wanted to play at Satanism to add color to their parties. But no, they're the real deal.

You need to understand, I've seen things over the years. Been at their rituals, seen the results of their practices. They are calling on truly evil, primordial forces to gain wealth and kill their enemies. To grasp a kind of power that makes them more than human. By the time I really realized what I had gotten into, it was too late.

****

"Okay, but what're the dolls actually for?"

Teddy nodded. "I'm getting to that." He stood up and walked to the fireplace in the room. "The first thing you need to accept is that Hell is real. There are other worlds, other realms, than this one, and Hell is one of them. It is much different now than it once was, but its purpose is largely the same. It is a terrible place for terrible souls."

He turned to look at me with a humorless smile. "Unsurprisingly, my associates fall into that category. And as I feared…as was confirmed for me this week…so do I." He sighed. "And none of us want to go there. So one of the biggest goals of any high-level black magic hoodooer is to find a loophole or an escape hatch, a way of cheating the consequences of playing with those dark forces. There aren't many, but the dolls are one of them. If they are made correctly and the ritual is done right, the person and the doll swap places, sending the doll to Hell."

I shook my head. "Let's say I believe all this is real, which I don't. Aren't you just delaying the inevitable? I mean, you're still going to die again eventually, right?"

He wobbled his hand back and forth. "Yes and no. When you brought me back, I came back in a new body. Basically, a physical manifestation of my spiritual and mental self-image. That can lead to some fucked up results at times, but for most people they come back in a relatively healthy version of their normal body, as most people see the thing that killed them or the infirmities they have as separate from themselves. So the plaque-laden artery that killed me is likely clean as a whistle now."

"Also, if they can get a few hours back here, many of them can heal themselves. And they can extend their lives for quite some time as well. I think Darrow was well over a hundred when I first met him, and he's still around now."

"But the biggest thing is that they are all biding their time for something they call the Breach. They don't talk to me about it, but the snatches I've heard make it sound like it's something they think will change the rules for them. Either way, they would rather be here than in Hell." He rubbed his chest absently. "I share the sentiment."

I was going to ask another question when there was a loud knock on the front door. Teddy raised his finger to his lips. "Stay here. If you hear me say the phrase…'worth my salt', you run out the back. Run and keep running, and don't go home. Never go back to places they could find you." He waved his hand placatingly at my expression. "Hopefully it won't be needed though. They need me too much."

I could see he was worried, and while I wasn't sure how much of what he was saying was true, I did trust I was in serious danger. I heard him open the front door in the middle of a louder knock. A voice that sounded like the lawyer I had met that morning echoed down the hall.

"We know she didn't leave, Ted. I'm sorry, but we have to take her."

Part Three

"Hershel, I think enough of your intelligence to assume that you know that's not going to happen. My niece is staying with me and is under my protection. She's not going to blab your precious secrets, because she's intelligent and not suicidal. So are we good?"

I heard a chuff of what sounded like irritated disbelief from the other man. "No, Ted. We're not 'good'. You need to remember your place. You are only important because we find you useful. You have no power on your own. Now step aside."

Uncle Teddy's voice was lower but icy when he spoke next. "You know, I could tell you to go to Hell, but coming from me, it'd be less of an insult and more of a sentence, wouldn't it? Because trust me when I tell you that if you or any of the rest of the Circle decide to start trying to treat me as a pet instead of a partner, your safety net will be revoked permanently. And maybe they'll find someone to replace me in another fifty or sixty years — that is how long ya'll looked the last time, right?"

"But how long do you think your old, stinking asses have before your hoodoo can't keep you going any longer? Before something gets you that you didn't see coming? A brain aneurysm, a car accident, or shit, a high-powered round through your fat head from 200 yards away? Because the magic only works on things you or your minions can see and anticipate, right? Right."

"Now me, I don't have any fancy magic like that. I'm just a simple dollmaker, and like you said, I have to remember my place. It seems to me, if I had any sense, any sense at all, I'd take some of the millions of dollars ya'll have kindly paid me over the years to put out contingency contracts on all of my associates in case someone decided to try to step on my neck one day. Take me down from a simple dollmaker to somebody's cur dog. Why, if I had a brain in my head, I'd tell them that if they hear I'm dead and don't get a correction from me personally within a week, they should take revenge on whoever did it. And since those fellas—and ladies, I would assume—are assassins, not detectives, and because I'm just a simple dollmaker not sure of who would ever want to do me harm, I'd tell them to just complete all the contracts to make sure they got the right one."

When Myers spoke next, his voice was shaking and pleading. "We would never hurt you…you're our friend and we do need you, of course. But she has to go! This isn't coming from me. It's from the top."

My uncle gave a short laugh. "See, the problem with that is I just updated my contracts twenty minutes ago. Cost a bit extra, but that's okay. Worth it to see my family safe. If anything happens to my niece or her family, same rules apply. You're right about one thing though, Hershel. You are my friend. You all are. And so I'm just going to forget this happened at all. You just came by to visit tonight, right? To say hey."

There was a stretch of silence and Ted's voice was as hard and cold as river rocks when he spoke next. "I said, isn't that right, Hershel."

"Um, yeah. That's right." The other man sounded utterly defeated now.

"Good. I'd love to hang around and chat, but I still have some preparations to finish for the big party on Saturday. So while I won't tell you to go to Hell, I will tell you to fuck off." I heard the door slam and then Uncle Teddy was coming back in, a grim smile on his face.

"That bought us some time at least. We'll see how much."

I went cold. "Time? As in, you think they're still going to try and get me?"

He raised an eyebrow. "Oh yeah. Definitely. Aside from being crazy and evil, they're also used to getting their way. They are scared to go against me directly too hard, and while they might decide to just try and enslave me, they would much rather placate or scare me into submission. But that won't stop them from wanting to get rid of you, both to silence you and to show me that I'm their dog after all. Tonight will set them back though, and they'll likely waste a day or two debating and arguing over what to do next."

I glanced at the dark windows in the room nervously. "What's to stop them from just killing me with a spell or sending a monster in after me if they have all this power?"

He nodded. "A good thought, but it wouldn't work. Over the years I've made more than one doll in exchange for services. There are layers of wards protecting this house that are beyond what could be stripped away in a month, much less a few days. Nothing magical gets in or out of this house unless I invite it to enter or leave personally."

"Okay. Well, that's good. But what're we going to do?"

"We aren't going to do anything. You're going to go cut me off an inch of your hair and then go to bed in one of the guest rooms. Do not leave this house under any circumstances until I tell you to, okay?"

I frowned. "Okay…but why my hair?" I tried to smile. "Planning on making me a doll too?"

He didn't return the smile. "Well, yes. Of course. For a variety of reasons, but the most salient to you being that most likely, if you die any time in the next few weeks, you're going to Hell."

I felt the dull roar of panic building in my ears. "What are you talking about? Why would I go to Hell? I'm not a bad person."

Teddy sighed. "You have to stop looking at it as black and white or right and wrong. There are rules for how you get sent to Hell and how you get out. Because you can get out without using a cheat like the dolls, but it usually takes several hundred or thousands of years. But I digress. The point is that you did an infernal ritual tonight and violated the rules of Hell in the process. You didn't know what you were doing, so that helps a bit, but you'll still carry a…stain around for awhile. The good news is that something isolated like that fades after a bit. If you died a few months from now, all would likely be fine. If you got hit by a bus tomorrow…well, I'd lay odds that you're going to Hell."

"So you're going to make me a doll for in case I get sent to Hell."

He smiled thinly. "Yep. There are scissors in the bathroom. Underlayers are fine, not trying to make you look like a mental patient."

****

For most of the next day, Uncle Teddy was holed up in his workshop working on my doll and other "preparations." He said my doll was going to be extra special, so he had to take more time than usual to get everything just right. Apparently the other preparations were for a party he was throwing on Saturday.

Teddy told me that months earlier he had sent out invitations to everyone he made dolls for. The group he knew locally called themselves the Circle, but there were Circles all over the world, and over the years, he had dealt with many of them. He had billed the party as largely a get-together, where people from different Circles could come together and socialize for an evening without any ceremony or ritual to be performed. But the real draw was that he was giving every guest in attendance an updated version of their doll.

He said that in the early years since making that first doll, he had made it a priority to learn Latin and French — as well as a few other languages that came up in texts he ran across. The pursuit of more knowledge about the memoriam dolls was partially out of curiosity and a desire to keep improving at his craft through greater understanding. But it was also out of a strong sense of self-preservation. He wanted to know where all the emergency exits were. So he surreptitiously became one of the foremost experts in the world on the hellbound effigies he was making.

One thing that he learned was that the dolls had a shelf life. They were like a snapshot of the person at the time they were created, and the longer the time between the doll's creation and the person dying and being sent to Hell, the longer it would take for the ritual to bring them back. Time was much faster in Hell and out-of-sync with our reality, so an old doll could turn a week into a month or a year or a decade.

This worked out well for him, as he had frequent repeat customers. But it also meant that a gift like he was offering was especially prized. He expected the party to be pretty packed, and when I asked him why he was still having it considering everything that was going on, he looked at me incredulously.

"People have already RSVP'd."

****

I don't trust my Uncle Teddy, in part because I don't really know him, and in part because I'm starting to believe what he's telling me is actually true. I have to admit though, he is a talented artist. When he showed me my doll, I was amazed by it. It was slightly different than the others, with a larger head than the ones he had lining a back room in preparation for the party. Still, it was unmistakably me. Touching the doll's face, I felt a stirring of disquiet. By being around him, by having my own doll made, wasn't I just further securing a place in Hell?

Still, I felt like I needed the insurance policy. And whatever my misgivings, I did believe that Teddy was looking out for me.

"Why did you give me that children's book with the poem about Hell in it when I was little? It freaked me out."

We were sitting in a large, oak-paneled dining room eating frozen pizza. He looked weary from his non-stop work of the last few hours, but he seemed cheerful as well, and when I asked the question, his laughter was genuine.

"Shit, yeah, sorry about that. I...I've had some dark, lonely times doing this for them. I distanced myself from all of you because I didn't want them touching your lives. But then I realized that they didn't want me having any friends here either. Their precious fucking secrecy."

"Now, they never told me what to do, you understand. They didn't want to piss me off. But if I made a friend, dated someone, fuck, even hired a prostitute, they would suddenly drop off the face of the earth. After a couple of years of that I gave up."

He stared down at his pizza, his face sagging with the weight of his past and his pain. When he looked back up, his lips carried a sad smile. "I was there when you were born. Did you know that? You were a beautiful baby." He pushed the plate away from himself and sat back. "When I realized I would never be around ya'll, and that I'd never be allowed to have a family of my own, I got very down. They kept close watch on me to make sure I didn't become suicidal, but there were still a couple of times when I considered it."

"What got me through it was thinking about you. About you growing up, living a good and full life, having a family of your own maybe. You almost became like a surrogate daughter to me in my daydreams."

He sighed, looking slightly embarrassed. "I found that poem in my research on the dolls. It was in a journal kept by a Germanic occultist in the late 17th century. In one of my more maudlin moments, I bought you that book and wrote the poem in it. Why? I couldn't really say, to be honest. Maybe as a warning or a cry for help. I felt like I knew you in my own pathetic way, and that poem was the closest I've ever come to telling anyone about what is going on." He frowned, his face growing dark. "About the fucking trap I've put myself in."

I reached forward and awkwardly patted his hand. "We'll figure something out."

He looked a little like I had punched him in the stomach as he drew his hand away. "I'm sorry, but I told you, it's not we. And I've already got it figured out."

His voice was starting to sound strange and far away, and I realized with a surge of panic that my vision was warped and fading as well. Had he drugged me? Had the fucker actually drugged me?

I tried to stand, but it was like trying to walk on marbles. Every movement sent me into a staggering slow-motion dance of overcorrections until I plopped back into the chair again. On my third try I managed to stay on my feet, and I looked over at my uncle. He was watching me silently, his eyes sad and glimmering. Somehow his emotion made it more real and terrifying. I had to get out of here now before it was

The overhead lights glared down at me like half a dozen angry small suns, every one of them intent on boring through my eyelids and into my aching brain. Wincing, I eased my eyes open and tried to look around. I was in a large cinderblock room of some sort, possibly some kind of workshop, as I saw a variety of tools and saws hanging on one wall.

As I came back to myself a little more, I realized with growing panic that I was strapped down to a table or bench of some kind. I could move my head, but that was all. I started to scream, but a voice to my right quickly silenced me.

"There, there," Dilly said, her dry cooing sounding like the rustle of a snake shedding its skin, "Quit making such a fuss." The old woman came into my field of view and I saw she looked much the same as she had at the wake, though she was now wearing casual clothes underneath a long, black rubber apron. "Milly over there thinks we should keep you alive. Amputate your limbs, of course, but keep you alive in case we need to bring back that Uncle of yours again. She's afraid that the blood won't work if you aren't still breathing."

She smiled, her yellow, crooked teeth peeking out behind her lips like decaying gravestones. "Now for my part, I've looked at a great many of the old texts and I don't think it's required. I think we can drain you, store the blood, and not have to worry about you eating and shitting between now and the Breach."

She shook her head with mock sorrow. "But that Milly, she's as stubborn a lady as I've ever known. I'd about given up on convincing her to slit you like a hog and drain you dry. But," she leaned closer to me conspiratorially, "you keep making a racket like that…well, she might be persuaded yet. So go ahead if you want. Go ahead and scream."

<u>**Part Four**</u>

"Let's just ask him."

Dilly's upper lip raised like a snarling dog at Milly's suggestion. "No. Why? Do you think he knows more than I do?"

Milly had been sitting in the corner of the room, but now she stood up and approached Dilly. "No, of course not. He's nothing compared to us. Compared to you." She brushed her hand down the other old woman's cheek. "But you have to admit, he has the gift. We've had fourteen successful recoveries out of fourteen attempts since we brought him into our employ. You know how rare that is, and you know that kind of gift comes with a certain…intuition."

"I don't know that I would call all fourteen a complete success." A new, unfamiliar voice echoed from behind my view. The voice was watery and indistinct, as though someone was talking while drowning, as strange an idea as that was. I sensed movement and couldn't suppress a scream when the thing came into view.

Half of its face was human, though patchy and scaled over in spots. The other half was a ruin of gray-green twisted with contours like a mountain range on some alien world. Worse, that side of his face was always in subtle motion as several small crimson worms moved ceaselessly between dark pockets in the flesh. The man creature was wearing a sweatshirt, but poking out of one arm hole was something that looked more like a petrified tree branch than any kind of working hand. Still, as I watched, the monster hand flexed and moved, the skin splitting in a dozen places with every motion, leaking some dark corruption for a moment before healing back again. I tried to turn away, but Dilly grabbed my face and held me fast with surprising strength.

"You just keep making noises, don't you? Interrupting. And now you've been rude to my brother. I think exsanguination is the only real answer here."

Milly stepped forward. "Dilly, stop." She turned to look at the monster. "Peter, your…changes were due to your predilections, not a flaw with Teddy or your doll. We've been over this. You…overindulged in certain things, didn't you? And they became a part of you."

The creature called Peter took a couple of threatening steps towards Milly with a crooked gait. "You need to shut up now." He turned to look at his sister. "Dilly, you need to shut her up before I lose control."

But Milly pressed on. "You felt ashamed of your vices, didn't you? Ashamed of what you had become. You thought of yourself as a monster, so that's what you became. It's your fault, no one else's."

He let out a bellow of rage and raised his fist to strike Milly, but suddenly he froze still.

"You'd raise a hand to me? Even at your best you were not our equal." Peter flew back as though he had been shoved, his body sounding like it bounced off a far wall out of view before landing with a thud. Dilly let out a small cry and ran over to him.

"How could you? You know how he gets. He's very sensitive about what happened to him. About his…urges. You were goading him."

Milly's expression was hard. "No, I'm just tired of treating him like the baby he acts like. He's not dead. But I won't have him getting in our way with his tantrums any longer, you understand? You control him or next time I'll pull his head off like a maypop." She reached into a pocket and pulled out her cell phone. "And I'm calling Teddy. I'm tired of coddling you as well."

My head was swimming with everything I had just seen, and I was trying to simultaneously process it all while searching for some way out of this. Then I heard Uncle Teddy's voice over the speakerphone.

"Hey there, Millicent. How's my favorite girl?"

Milly's face had changed as soon as she had dialed his number, and it brightened further at his words. "Oh hush, you flirt. I'm doing good. Just here trying to decide what to do with your wayward niece. I'm afraid to kill her, but Dilly thinks it will be fine as long as we store the blood properly."

There was a brief pause before he answered. "Well, I'm not the expert, of course, so I'm just going with my gut here. But I think Cordelia is right on this one. In fact, I think it might be a mistake to keep her alive. Every time we've done the ritual, the blood kin was a willing participant. I'd be afraid that if she's forced to participate or still alive at all, her contrary intent might taint the offering. Where as if she's dead, the offering becomes neutral with no intervening or contrary will to counterbind it."

Dilly had walked back into view, her hands stained with more of the black ichor perpetually dripping from her brother. "That's what I said. But you know Milly, she's always so hard headed."

Teddy was giving a light laugh when Milly cut him off. "Teddy, how do you know about counterbound offerings?"

His laughter trailed off. "What? Oh, Darrow gave me a couple of books over the years. My foreign language skills aren't quite up to snuff, but I've made out a little of it. Did I use the term wrong?"

Milly's brow was still furrowed, but then Teddy spoke up again. "I wish you wouldn't tease me, Millicent. I know I don't know much, but I do try to learn from all of you." His voice sounded hurt and slightly petulant. It made Milly smile again.

"No, Teddy, you are a gift to us all. I'm sorry, I wasn't trying to tease you. And you used the term just fine." Dilly was rolling her eyes and Milly shot her a dark look. "You've been of great help to us in this too. And thank you again for telling us about Myers. I always knew there was something about that man. Very off-putting."

My uncle's voice was warm again. "Yeah, I just hate it came to that. He was my friend for years, but there's no way I could go along with what he was suggesting. For my sake and for yours." He let out a small sigh. "Anyway, on to happier topics. Ya'll going to be here tomorrow night for the party, right?"

Milly grinned wider, her cheeks coloring. "We wouldn't miss it for anything."

"Good, good. Say, is my niece there?"

She laughed, looking down at me. "Oh, she's here. If looks could kill, as they say. I think she's a tiny bit miffed with you."

Uncle Teddy chuckled slightly. "I bet. Hey, Cora. Sorry it worked out this way, but that's the way it goes sometimes, yeah? I wish you'd left like you were supposed to. It's kind of your fault you're in this mess, and now these nice ladies have to clean up behind you." I thought he was finished, but then he went on. "Still, I meant what I said. You were a nice little girl. When you get where you're going, remember that poem I wrote you. If you feel yourself getting too scared, say it and maybe it'll make you feel a bit better." Another pause and then, "Milly, I've got caterers beating down my door wanting to do prelim setup, so I have to go. See ya'll tomorrow night!"

When Milly hung up, Dilly started back in on her immediately.

"I don't trust that slick little fucker. Not one bit."

It was Milly's turn to roll her eyes. "I don't see why not. To the extent anyone is trustworthy, he's shown himself to be pretty reliable. When Myers approached him at the door and Teddy didn't turn this one over right away, when he supposedly threatened all of us, I admit I was a bit concerned as well." Dilly let out a snort, but Milly ignored it and continued. "But when he called me and told me about what Myers had suggested--Teddy letting him come back the next day to get and keep the girl, so he could gain standing and leverage over the rest of us...well, I didn't believe it at first either. But then Teddy promised to turn her over to us." She gestured towards me. "And there the girl lay, delivered like a holiday turkey."

Scowling, Dilly wagged a finger at the other woman. "Convenient. And Myers was a slime, but he didn't have the balls to do this. To go against all of us? Please."

Milly shrugged. "Well, I'd say you should go ask him, but..."

Dilly's frown deepened. "And that's another thing. He just happens to kill himself the next day? His doll destroyed and scattered next to his body? We don't do suicide, particularly without a doll in place. That kind of defeats the whole purpose of all this Teddy bullshit. So how does that make sense?"

Milly glared at her. "He was a drug addict. A pillhead. Had been for several years now. And shockingly, that's what he used to kill himself. Who knows why he did it? Maybe he was crazy or hopped up. I don't care. What I do care about is keeping our dollmaker somewhat happy and keeping him around for a long time. So just take the win. We got the girl. We're going to kill her like you wanted. Now just shut up and let's get to work."

Dilly retreated slightly under Milly's gaze, finally nodding reluctantly. "Fine. I hope you're right. Not that you care, but Peter's back is broken. It will probably take a month for it to regenerate fully."

Milly grabbed her arm, her tone softer. "I'm sorry about that. But he does have to learn not to get in our way. Now let's get her drained and get some sleep. Tomorrow is a big day."

****

"You know, Hell isn't what it's cracked up to be anymore. It's a lot worse." Dilly wasn't looking at my face, instead watching the lines they had put in my arms slowly pull the blood from my body. It had hurt at first, and they weren't gentle about it, but now I felt like I was floating. They had moved on to the third container in collecting the blood, and I had a feeling I would be dead soon. Milly had left to attend to something else after they had the process started, and some men had come in and drug Peter the monster out soon thereafter. So it was just me and Dilly, and she had decided to lecture me on the place I was heading to so soon.

"When Hell was first created, some of its first inhabitants were fallen angels, with Lucifer in charge for the most part. He set up the first kingdom of Hell, and it was remarkably orderly in its way. But then something new came to Hell."

"This new creature…it didn't want order or a kingdom. It just wanted to hunt and kill. The demons and other denizens of Hell, they started to fear it more than Lucifer. They called it the Hunter. No one knew much about it. There were rumors that it had been exiled into Hell from another realm by an entity called the Baron, but it was all frightened whispers in the dark. What Lucifer knew for sure was that it was killing his strongest demons and they weren't coming back."

"Because that's supposed to be the deal in Hell, right? You can be tortured and killed, but you always come back, ready for more. Not if the Hunter got you though. You were just gone--to where, no one knew, but its safe to say its as bad or worse than the place you just left. Because the Hunter's methods may be simple, but he is not. He's not a dumb animal and he's not easily tricked. As Lucifer found out."

"Lucifer tracked the Hunter easily--he wasn't trying to hide, and wherever he went, the landscape changed into dark and terrible woods. But this wasn't concerning to Lucifer. It was still his realm overall, and he wielded considerable power there. He set traps, he summoned armies, and he prepared himself for battle. And then he started to sing."

Even in my light-headed state, my expression must have looked confused, because Dilly gave me a small, cold smile.

"Oh, I know what you're thinking. But music has a great deal of power, and Lucifer was skilled in its use. It's thought that he intended to trap the Hunter in the magic of his song and then bring the full weight of Hell down on top of him until he was wholly obliterated. But Lucifer was used to fighting other angels and tormenting souls. He didn't understand what the Hunter really was, because no one did. And that's what killed him."

"The Hunter walked through his song like it was nothing. He flung aside the Devil's armies until the few demons that were left fled in terror. Then it was just Lucifer, the brightest angel, blazing on top of a hill of skulls and rotting flesh, ready to face down the usurper." Dilly looked almost star-struck at the image, crazy hag that she was. "But…it didn't work. The Hunter was faster and stronger than him. More powerful. His infernal magics barely had any effect at all on the creature, yet his flesh would begin to wither at the Hunter's touch. Time is a strange thing in Hell, or so I've heard, but by all accounts it was a short fight. And in the end, Lucifer's fire was extinguished."

I had started to fade out and Dilly slapped me hard. "Wake up. Don't be rude. I'm giving you facts about your impending destination before you land." She let out a nasty chuckle. "So you can appreciate it more. The least you can..." I tried to keep my eyes open, but everything was so far away now. And then I was

****

in a dark forest. The sound of ice cracking on branches echoed off to my left and I jumped, looking out into the fog and trees that faded into blackness in every direction. I was naked, but my body seemed healthy and whole. But the air was freezing, and as I stood up, I winced in pain at the rocks biting into my bare feet.

Shivering, I tried to look up past the trees for stars or moonlight, but there was nothing. I listened out for any kind of noise, but the only sound was the stark wind cutting through the trees above me. It made the leaves tremble and rattle, and the sound made me feel utterly terrified and alone. I didn't know what to do. Where to go. I thought about just sitting back down where I was, as at least I wasn't being attacked so far staying here... but then I heard it.

Whistling. High, clear notes from someone whistling as they approached me from out in the dark. Somehow that sound was a thousand times worse than the trees or the cold or anything in my imagination. I understood at my soul's core that it was the train whistle of unending pain and oblivion.

So I ran. And the thing behind me followed.

Part Five

It didn't matter how fast I tried to run, the whistling kept growing closer. My feet were already slick with blood from pounding across the rocky ground that lay between the trees, and my arms and face were covered by a dozen scratches. It felt like the branches were reaching out to me as I passed, and perhaps they were, but I saw no way to avoid them. There was nothing but trees and fog and dark in this place, and while I wasn't growing tired, I knew I was losing ground.

Then I saw what looked like a dim light in the distance. I had no idea whether it was a good sign or not — the idea of finding any kind of help or safe haven in Hell seemed unlikely — but at least it was something new, and it was hard to imagine it making things much worse. I veered to my right and headed toward what I could now see was flickering firelight, though the flames were a sickly green color that sent weak shafts of illumination between the trees as I approached. The whistling was even closer now, but I had forced myself to slow down and look at the figures surrounding the campfire.

Hiding near the edge of the light, I peered around the thick trunk of a tree at the small group gathered at the camp. I had no real point of reference, but they looked like they might be demons. All of them were twisted and monstrous, and while they all looked dangerous--some with ragged claws and others with dozens of tooth-filled slashes in their flesh that smacked hungrily in the dancing firelight--they all looked somewhat broken and sad too. It sounds strange to try and apply human emotions and behaviors to such alien creatures, but dejection and fear came off them like a stench, and every time the wind blew hard or ice cracked somewhere out in the dark, several of them would jump and look around uneasily.

I had the thought that I was surprised they hadn't gotten spooked by the whistling, but then I realized the whistling was gone, and its absence wasn't a comfort. Whatever had been making that tune was still here. I could feel it.

I almost went out to the group of monsters, both to warn them and to hopefully get safety in their numbers, but that's when I noticed that they were cooking something on the fire. It was a pair of human children. I sucked in a deep breath, deciding to sneak away and keep moving, and that's when I saw something at the perimeter of the firelight on the far side of the camp.

It was me. Or at least something that looked like me. Its eyes were glowing in the green light, and I realized with mounting horror that it wasn't looking at the demons or the roasting children. It was looking at me. I was about to bolt when the other Cora gave me a smile and put a finger to her lips in a shushing gesture while shaking her head.

Then she was on them, moving like a blur and ripping into the half dozen creatures despite their large size and fearsome appearance. She wouldn't kill them outright, not at first. She would maim them each in turn, crippling them enough that they could only crawl or stagger away from the light into the forest. Like wounded deer, they scattered in every direction, and my mirror self let them, licking her gore-soaked hand idly as though waiting for something.

Time passed, and then suddenly she was gone in a blur. A few moments later I heard an inhuman howl far in the distance. Then a second, a third, more…until all of the demonic campers had been tracked down and dealt with. It was hard to gauge time here, even in my head, but after the second scream I had begun to run. It didn't seem I made it far before the last scream began, and within a short while I was hearing the whistling again. Closer this time and gaining fast.

I cast my gaze in every direction. There were no more landmarks, no more fires. Just deep, dark…Fuck. The poem! What was the poem? I didn't know if I could trust Uncle Teddy's suggestion, but I was out of options.

My voice sounded strange and hollow in my own ears as I began. "Hell is a forest both dark and deep…" Shit, that wasn't right. And the whistling was almost on top of me now. "Hell is a forest deep and dark. Its ground is…fuck. Hell is a forest deep and dark. Its earth is cold, its trees are stark. Among the shades dwells the Hunter's face…" My feet left the ground as I was shoved hard from behind and slammed into a tree. I slid down its surface with a grunt, my back burning where I had been touched. I looked up to see the Hunter, still wearing my face, walking up with a smile.

"Please send another in my place!"

Everything blurred and I felt like I was floating for a moment before landing back on the rocky ground with a groaning thud. I lifted my eyes, expecting to see the Hunter still coming toward me, but it was gone. Or rather, I was. I was still in the forests of Hell, but it was a different spot. To the left I could hear the roar of what sounded like a waterfall, and under that sound, what might have been the soft notes of a violin being played.

Teddy had bought me some time at least. Hopefully it would take some time for the Hunter to…

There was a blur of motion and it was back in front of me again. It wasn't smiling any longer, and its anger, even using my expressions, was a terrible sight, pulling a discordant wail from my throat as I scrabbled back. I was ready to give up, to give in. There was no beating this thing or running from it. All I had done was piss it off. I kept moving backwards in an awkward crabwalk, scraping up my hands as I went, but I was out of options.

The Hunter moved toward me, its hand outstretched as it drew near. But then it was gone. The Hunter had just vanished into thin air. I sobbed with relief at first, slowly standing on shaky knees, but then I let out a scream. Laying where the Hunter had been was a burning doll.

The burning doll was mine.

****

"Ladies and gentleman, if I can have your attention please." Standing on a low table in one corner of the room, I looked out across the gathered assembly of some of the most powerful dark magic users in the world. Most of them were old and ugly. You would think that performing the blackest of black magic rituals, potentially condemning yourself to eons in Hell (or worse if the rumors of the Hunter were true), would at least come with some guarantee of being young and hot. But no, while there were a few people that normally stood out from the crowd, here in my magic no fly zone, they looked as old, fat and homely as the rest. There was more than one black velvet muumuu in attendance, I can tell you that much, as well as several Victorian silk chokers that looked like wrappings around a turkey's neck.

The reason, of course, was that they were without their glamours and enchantments. They had none of the tricks and trappings that they used to deceive others, none of the powers that gave them their air of superiority and their ability to control and ruin lives. What you were left with was something that looked vaguely like a goth threw up on a nursing home.

Still, they were all supremely dangerous. Intelligent and vicious sociopaths, they were more than capable of killing me if I didn't play my part just right. And that would mean not only condemning me, but poor Cora, to Hell for a much longer period of time.

So I had smiled and chatted all night. Told jokes and acted friendly. I could tell some still viewed me with suspicion, but most had been mollified by my turning over Cora. They were all so arrogant, so used to getting their way, that the idea of "the dollmaker" betraying them seemed as alien as finding a dog reading a newspaper. But that's the problem. Just because you don't see something or think it's possible doesn't have any real bearing on what is or isn't real. And you never really know what that dog is up to when you're not looking.

"I gathered you here tonight in a celebration of all our years together." A scattering of applause from the crowd, and then I went on. "As you know, I've painstakingly crafted you all new dolls as parting gifts tonight. A way of paying you back for all you've given me." This time the applause was much louder and lasted some time before fading away.

"You've given me horror. Loneliness. Guilt. And a blot on my soul I might never be able to wash away. Though my hope is that tonight will be a good start." The herd was looking confused and nervous now, glancing at each other questioningly. I pushed on before they could start interrupting.

"A couple of unique features about this house. This room, where I was brought back from Hell just days ago, is replicated on the floor below us and the floor above us. There, as here, only two doors lead into the room and both have a reinforced titanium core. There, as here, those doors were locked ten minutes ago." Now the crowd was murmuring, confusion turning to anger as people started shouting questions. What was the meaning of this, etc. Typical poutiness from arrogant people starting to smell their own end.

"Now, in the room below us, large logs of the ritual wood we use for our little "undo" rituals have been set in the proper pattern and soaked in gasoline. They'll be ignited on a timer in five minutes. In the room above us, are all of your new dolls. Painstakingly made, as I said. Crafted with care. Do you know how hard it was to get right? I had to make the dolls close enough to perfect that it would bind you to them but just off enough that they wouldn't actually bring you back."

The partygoers were largely silent now. Listening and

calculating. I needed to wrap this up soon. "As some of you may know, you only get one shot at being brought back from Hell with a doll. If the doll bound to you is flawed, or if the ritual itself gets messed up…well, you're going to have a bad time. So when your new dolls burn, you won't be coming back again. Ever."

"Now, I know what you're thinking. Just rush me and kill me, find a way to thwart my plan. Or try and call for help, getting some of the guards and drivers waiting dutifully outside to break you out before the fire and smoke reaches this level. Both solid ideas. Which is why we have this." I pulled a gun out of a small holster at the back of my waist, "And this." I kicked the top off a large hatbox that sat on the table next to me.

"The gun is obvious. You rush me, I shoot you in the face. I can't kill all of you with the gun, but I have a sneaking suspicion that your individual threshold for altruism and teamplay is pretty low, and wouldn't it suck to be the one who gets the bullet?" I smiled at the crowd, feeling the waves of hatred and fear baking off them like heat. "The box is less obvious, so allow me to explain. Inside it is another, much smaller, ritual site with only one doll in it. It's a very special doll made for someone very special. Or, if I'm being totally accurate, two very special someones. You'll get to meet one of them when I set it on fire. You may have heard of them. They're called the Hunter."

Nervous laughter rippled through the room. These idiots had decided this was all some strange practical joke. But among them I saw a few terrified looks from those that were starting to understand what I had done.

I brought out a lighter, summoning the flame and tossing it in the box with Cora's doll with one motion. I then put the gun to my temple.

"I really don't want to be here when the Hunter arrives,

so this is where I take my leave. See you bitches in Hell."

And then I pulled the trigger.

****

I tried to put my doll out, though I wasn't sure for what purpose, but there was nothing to extinguish it with. I thought about the sound of the waterfall nearby, and while it seemed unlikely I could get any real amount of water to the doll in time, it was burning too fiercely for me to pick it up. With no better option, I started heading toward the waterfall with the idea of trying to carry water cupped in my hands if I could, but I only made it a handful of steps before I saw a naked Teddy jogging in my direction.

"Cora! Long time no see. Looking well-ish." He tried to smile, but it faltered and fell from his face quickly. "Look, I know this has all been terrifying, and I'm very glad you're okay. I'm sorry you've gotten pulled into all this, but it's almost over. I'd hug you, but we're both naked, and I'm not that kind of uncle. So for now just come over here and wait with me."

I wanted to be angry with him, but honestly the relief at seeing someone familiar overwhelmed every other emotion for the moment. I nodded numbly and went with him a few yards distant behind a thick tree. He smiled again, this time more genuinely, and gave me a wink. "Hard to judge the time here, but I don't think it'll be too long."

After what felt like a few minutes, naked people started appearing out of thin air. First one or two, then in several larger batches before slowing down to a trickle. Most of them were older looking, and I realized that I recognized several of them from my uncle's wake. Even better, I saw that Milly and Dilly were among them. I gave my uncle a questioning look and he nodded, whispering, "The Hunter is making short work of them. In our world, if it kills them they go to Hell. In Hell, if it kills them…well, no one knows where they go. Speaking of which, our friend the Hunter will be back here shortly. Do not run when you see it. I think it'll be busy with our friends there long enough to buy us the time we need."

As if summoned by his words, the Hunter, now flickering between the appearances of the nearly three dozen people it had just killed, reappeared in the midst of their condemned souls. Every face it shifted to shared the same satisfied smile as it took them all in. They tried to run, but I saw it grab Dilly and tear her in half like tissue paper, her body disintegrating into a gray floating ash and then nothing. Milly let out a scream and the Hunter rounded on her as Teddy disappeared from next to me. I had time to feel a new swell of terror before my vision blurred and I found myself rolling off a table in Teddy's ritual room.

I landed in a thick carpet of broken bones and gore. Retching, I tried to stand but kept slipping back down into it. Finally. I managed to use the table as support to get up. I almost fell again when I saw Teddy's corpse laying on the table, a chunk of his head missing on one side.

The door on the far end of the room opened and Teddy came in, his new body whole but still disturbingly naked. He looked around the room and then at me. "Hey there, sunshine. You need a bath."

****

"So I guess I owe you an explanation or two."

I was freshly washed and scrubbed now, sitting in a large terrycloth robe on the sofa in Teddy's parlor. Teddy sat across from me, his expression serious and his tone sincere. It helped him not making a joke out of it anymore, but I was still confused, angry and scared.

"Yeah, you could say that."

He nodded. "Okay, well I'll start at the beginning. For

the last several years, going on almost a decade now, I've been studying and planning a way to get rid of them. Permanently. I didn't want to just kill them, as I know enough to know some of them might find another way out of Hell. So the obvious solution was to ensure the Hunter got them all quickly, sending them to wherever it sends them. When I had most everything ready, I killed myself." I went to ask a question, but he was already shaking his head. "Yeah, the whole stroke thing, not true. I had that set up to hide the fact that it was planned. I needed to get to Hell to pick up the last ingredient I needed for my plan. Hair from the Hunter."

Now I did interrupt. "How did you get hair from the Hunter without getting killed yourself?"

"Well, I didn't get it from the Hunter. I got it from a demon I'd been in contact with that thought I could get him out of Hell. Demons are not big fans of Hell anymore as you might imagine."

I shuddered. "Yeah, I saw some of that firsthand."

He frowned. "I'm sorry for what you had to go through. I didn't intend for you to be a part of it at all past burning my doll, but when you stayed, I had to incorporate you into the plan as best I could. Anyway, the demon had gotten some of the Hunter's hair at some point--he claimed it was from the Hunter's final battle with Lucifer, but who knows really. He wanted to trade it for safe passage out, and when he saw I was lying to him, the bastard tried to gut me. I got away, but he was on my trail. Thankfully, you got me out when you did."

"Yeah, and your way of thanking me was to turn me over to those hags." I grimaced. "Your buddy Dilly is quite the Hell historian, so she told me some stuff about the Hunter too."

He sighed, rubbing his neck. "I know, I know. I'm sorry. But it really was necessary. I had to get them all here, and for that they had to still trust me, and the only way to regain their trust was to frame Myers and give you over. Plus, I knew I could get you back from Hell."

Glaring at him, I took a deep breath before speaking. "What exactly did you do to them?"

Teddy broke into a grin. "Now this is the good part. You know what a nesting doll is? It's those little dolls that have smaller versions of the doll inside it. That's essentially what your doll was. The head of the outer doll contained a smaller version, and that smaller version contained a tiny version. The outer doll was bound with the Hunter's hair, as was the smaller doll inside. The tiny doll at the center had your hair, as well as blood from me. I had no blood to put on the Hunter's doll other than mine or yours, so I used yours on a hunch--or my gifted doll intuition if you prefer. I already knew from talking to that demon that the Hunter liked to mirror its prey, so my hope was that your blood would act the same as kin blood for summoning the Hunter."

I frowned. "But how did you know the Hunter would be hunting and mirroring me?"

He winced. "I don't know a ton about the Hunter, but I know more than most. And the impression I've gotten is that it's pretty vindictive. It does not like people escaping Hell via the dolls. So I figured it would be after you pretty quick since you helped me escape already."

"So you guessed, and your best plan put me running from the Hunter for hours or days or whatever in Hell. It could have killed me, sent me somewhere you couldn't get me back from. Did you think about that?"

His expression grew dark. "Of course I did. I hated it. But killing these people, obliterating them from the face of Hell and Earth was more important than you or me. This isn't just about revenge. These people mean to break the universe. Tonight we took out some of their most powerful members, and if we got sacrificed along the way, so be it." He smiled thinly. "Still, we didn't, so yay for that. Now if I can finish explaining?"

I nodded sullenly. I saw his point, but I didn't like it. I could still feel the chill of those woods on my skin, and I was having a hard time not constantly peering into the shadowed corners of the room. With an effort, I pulled my focus back on what he was telling me.

"Okay, so I got them all here. I locked them in that room with me, lying and telling them I had the ritual pattern set in the floor below them and the dolls above them. In truth, the pattern and the dolls were both above. I did have charges set to detonate on the lower floor if we weren't back in a few minutes, but I didn't plan on burning down my house if I could avoid it, in part because I didn't want us returning to an inferno. But I was trying to hedge my bets. If the Hunter didn't get summoned, or if he worked slower than I anticipated in killing them all, I wanted any outside efforts by their people to be focused on getting them out and dousing the logs, not the explosives I had hidden or the ritual room I had set up above them. As it turned out, the Hunter did come and kill them after all, and the timed incendiary I had set upstairs to light the wood and dolls on the second floor was already burned out by the time we got back."

"But how did the dolls actually work this time?"

He shrugged. "Well, mine was like normal. I had gotten some blood from you before I turned you over, so I was set to get pulled back when mine burned. Theirs were all flawed-- they had no blood on them and had several other intentional imperfections, so once they burned, using the dolls to return became a dead end for my dear friends. As for yours, all the layers of dolls were carefully prepared to keep burning. I had to make sure it burned all the way through to the inner doll or you'd be stuck there with the rest of them. The outer doll burned and summoned the Hunter here, sending the doll to

Hell. The middle doll burned, summoning the Hunter back to Hell and bringing the doll back here. Finally, the inner doll burned, sending it back to Hell and pulling you back here." He sat back with a satisfied smile. "Make sense?"

I scowled at him. "Yeah. Shit. You were taking a lot of chances with all of this. I guess I get why, but fuck." I paused. "So is it over now? Really and truly done?"

His smile was cold now. "Oh, I'm not done yet. There are a lot more of these people out there, and they need to go. I've got the resources I need to make that happen, and a lot of atonement is going to be required if I have a chance of not winding up back in the forest some day. But for you, yeah, it's done. I'm going to be giving you a cashier's check for ten million dollars, and after you deposit that, you don't ever have to associate with me again."

I looked at him in stunned silence, not sure of what to say.

"Of course," he continued, his smile warmer now and his eyes dancing. "You could always stick around and help out your ol' Uncle Teddy."

Have you ever heard of the movie *"Die hungrige Klinge"*?

I've always loved movies, and when I got the chance last year to become a projectionist at the local small indie theater, I jumped at it. There wasn't much to the job, really. Despite the old-fashioned décor and stylized pretense, it was a fairly modern theater in most ways that mattered. Big, comfy seats, a soda machine where you could add your own flavors on a touchscreen, and a relatively new sound system.

One of the things it did have going for it though was it still had old-school projectors. So many places now have gone to purely digital projectors, but not the Phoenix. You had to load the big, ten-pound reels and switch between the two projectors when the time was right so there was no interruption in the film. Even that process was largely automated though, and what had seemed at the start like the first steps into some mysterious and arcane world of film quickly became the brain-dead monotony of making sure the machines kept working while half-watching the same old movie for the hundredth time.

Don't get me wrong, overall I loved the job, and a lot of the movies were either classics I had never seen or more obscure movies I had never heard of. Mr. Brubaker, the owner of the theater, was a kind man who had good taste in films but bad instincts when it came to business. The sleepy college town scene was good for repeat customers, but bad for big spenders, particularly when we made most of our money on concessions.

The problem was our theater wasn't the type you go to for the blockbusters or to hang out with your friends. Most of our audience members came as couples or by themselves, and they were there for the movie, not overpriced candy. I tried to suggest some ways we could make extra money, and one of them, Horror Movie Monday, actually worked. Some weeks we would make more money showing that double feature than we did the rest of the week combined.

But it wasn't enough, and I could tell Brubaker was worried about losing the place. That why when he asked me for a favor, I said yes.

He had been contacted by some kind of underground film group that I had never heard of. To be fair, the group didn't have a name, or if they did, I never knew it. But they had arranged with Brubaker via email to rent out the theater for one night from midnight until six in the morning. They said they were intending to show one movie, and it should only last approximately two hours, but they wanted the additional time for any clean-up that may be needed. They promised the theater would be left in the same condition as when they found it, and they required no staff other than a single projectionist.

As Brubaker told me about it, I felt a sinking feeling in the pit of my stomach. I worried he was being set up for a practical joke, or worse, being taken advantage of by some weirdos that would come in and trash the place. But then he told me with a beaming smile that they had paid $25,000.00 cash upfront through a courier. That was more than we made in three months, and he told me he'd give me $500.00 if I would stay the following night to run the projector for the group and keep an eye on things. Both for the money and to help him out, I agreed.

The next night, Brubaker went home about 11:30, making me promise to call at the first sign of trouble. I told him I would, but I doubted there would be any. I had half made up my mind that what they were showing was some kind of porno, and I had already decided where my line would be when it came to cleaning up anything they left behind. Brubaker would just have to take some of the money and hire a cleaning crew if things got overly sticky.

Still, the air of mystery around the whole thing had me excited, and I jumped slightly when I heard a hard knock on the front door. Glancing at the clock above the door, I saw it was exactly midnight.

When I opened the door, I almost burst out laughing. There were five figures outside, all dressed in dark robes with their heads covered and their faces obscured. As far as I know, the one in front is the only one that ever spoke. His voice was high and reedy, as though his words were being snatched away by some unseen wind as soon as he spoke them.

"You…ah…are the projectionist?"

I nodded. "Yes sir. I am. My name's Marshall."

He began moving into the lobby and I backed up to give more room as the others followed. "Your name is unnecessary, but we do need to know where to carry the film."

Swallowing, I smiled awkwardly and nodded. "Sure! Sure thing. Right this way." I turned to head toward the projectionist room when I heard a dry snapping sound behind me. It sounded like a brittle stick being broken in two, but I figured out it must be the leader snapping two bony fingers. Glancing back, I saw the other four hustling forward, each of them carrying a large metal case that I assumed contained the film reels.

The cases were different than anything I had ever seen, and I tried not to stare. Made out of what looked like a combination of ancient wood and banded metal, each film canister seemed to have been carved with a variety of figures and symbols. I never had the chance to study them in detail, but I could tell they each looked handmade and unique from one another, and I found myself wondering just how old this film must be, as though the age or appearance of the box would necessarily have anything to do with what it contained.

Once in the projectionist's room, I asked them which reels went first, but all I received was silence. When I went to reach for one of the boxes to see for myself, the figure I was approaching let out a strange hiss and stepped back. The other three moved in front of him and I found myself retreating, hands in the air. I was considering leaving all together, but once I had backed away a few steps, they set to opening the first two boxes and taking out strange reels that looked to be made of some kind of tarnished bronze. I was worried they wouldn't fit properly, but they had them ready to play within a matter of moments, working with an expertise and fluidity that amazed me.

I found myself wondering why I was there at all. If they weren't going to let me touch the film, and they knew how to work the projector, what was the point? Just then, I saw they had stepped back and were gesturing for me to start the projector. Frowning, I approached the projector, but then I hesitated.

Did they really want me to start now? Before anyone else showed up? Or was there anyone else coming anyway?

On a whim I glanced through the window to the theater below. My breath caught in my chest as I saw that nearly every seat was filled. While it was hard to tell from that distance and angle, it looked as though most of the people were dressed far more normally than my robed companions. I also saw more than one person looking up impatiently to where I stood. Ready to get the show started and get it over with, I hit the play button and started the film.

I can't describe what the film actually was, not really. I know I watched it, and I remember parts of it, but if I try focusing on the memory, it's like staring into the sun. I think my mind's eye will milk over and burn out before it lets me see.

I know the name of the film, I remember it from a black title card at the beginning. And I know there was blood and death…I'm not talking about in the film, though it may have been there too. I mean in the theater. I swear I remember seeing several audience members tearing each other apart as the movie played.

But my next clear memory, the first thing I knew that didn't hurt me, was locking up just after six that morning. I had done a final check of the theater as though I had just finished showing the children's Saturday matinee, and there were no signs that anyone had been there that night. It wasn't until I got home that I started shaking and crying.

This film has burrowed into me. I don't know anything about it, but I know it's wrong somehow. It's been almost a year since I saw it, and I can still feel it in me, pressing against my insides like a malignant cancer. I've tried forgetting about it, doping myself to sleep, exercising, drinking less and drinking more. Nothing has helped.

When I asked Brubaker about it, asked if he knew any more than he had told me, he just looked worried and slightly scared. He said he didn't, but he shouldn't have taken the money. He tried to get me to tell him what happened that night, wanted to know if they had hurt me somehow, and I just shook my head. Told him I couldn't talk about it, couldn't remember. Told him I had to quit working there because I had found a new job closer to my apartment. He just nodded, his eyes following me sadly as I waved good-bye and left. He knew I was lying…that I had no new job, but couldn't bear being in that place any longer. I hope he understood.

My last hope was that time would cure it, but it hasn't. Instead, whatever that movie did to me seems to be getting worse. I'm starting to lose time. Have strange thoughts. I've found myself drawn to repugnant things of late--rotten smells and yielding, decayed meat. It sickens me, yes, but it frightens me more.

I found your address through a friend of a friend--a man in Ontario that has apparently used you for some kind of...occult services in the past. I know this all may sound ridiculous to you, and if you are unable to help, I apologize for wasting your time. But if you can help, I will forever be in your debt. Because I think the movie is changing me.

It is called *"Die hungrige Klinge"*. I looked it up. It's German for "The Hungry Blade."

Please help me.

Signed, Marshall Abner

****

"We should help him."

Uncle Teddy looked at me warily over his glass of tea. He loved to drink dark, syrupy tea in the middle of the night, and in the last couple of weeks he had taken to waking me up to keep him company. Sometimes it amounted to little more than me transferring my sleep to the sofa while he stared into the fire, but tonight I couldn't get back to sleep and decided to go through some of the steadily accruing mail that he refused to look at. He claimed it was a precaution against hexes by post, but given the protections on his house, I knew that was unlikely.

"What do you mean?" His voice sounded mildly bewildered, but his expression reminded me of a fox watching a baby chick flop around in the straw.

"I mean we should help him. With this evil movie thing. Whatever it is."

Teddy rolled his eyes. "See, that's the first problem. You don't even know what it is. Yet you want to go rush off and 'help'." His elaborate air quotes were hampered by his death grip on the glass of tea.

I frowned at him. "Do you know what it is? Have you heard of The Hungry Blade?"

He took a long sip and sighed. "Yes, I have. By reputation only. It's very bad. And dangerous. It's a very bad and dangerous thing. So no. We should not help."

"But we might be able to…"

He raised a finger as he started to talk again. "No, and here's several reasons why not. First, I don't want to. Second, it could be a trap. Need I remind you that we have quite a few enemies after last month's party? This could just be them trying to lure us out. Third, fuck that guy. I don't know him, and neither do you. So fuck him. Fourth, if it is legit, he's already fucked. That movie is no joke. We're talking seriously spoopy shit. Fifth, I…why are you laughing at me, young lady?"

I calmed my laughter into a mild snicker. "Spoopy. You didn't even use it right. You really are super old, you know? And your other reasons are shit. You're just scared to leave the house. If your big plan to get rid of these evil occult types is to wait for them to die of old age, it's a sucky plan."

He gave me a sinister grin. "True. You've convinced me."

I felt a chill. "Just like that? Just that easy?"

He drained his glass with a satisfied smack, looking at it wistfully before turning back to me. "Just like that. I'm defenseless against your compelling arguments and stern reproach." He stood up with a stretch and a yawn. "Now let's go talk to the doomed boy. See if he knows any more about that spoopy movie before he croaks or turns into something Lovecrafty."

The Last Song of the Doomed Boy

Two things happened last night. I lost two hours of my life and I watched a young man get torn apart by a song.

Uncle Teddy made me drive on our trip to see the "doomed boy" Marshall Abner despite the fact we had two of his bodyguards with us. Their names were Perry and Max, though Teddy refused to call them by any names other than Heckle and Jeckle. When I had told him that I didn't get the reference, he acted offended and made me watch an hour of old cartoons centered around a pair of crows ("magpies," he corrected) that seemed to just be giant assholes ("whimsically aggressive towards authority," he opined). I still didn't get the joke, but at least Teddy was mollified enough by my penance to get into the car so we could go.

It was a four-hour drive, but I wasn't complaining. One thing we agreed on is that taking a plane was a bad idea at the moment. As Teddy said, "I don't care for the idea of being stuck in a metal tube at 30,000 feet with a pissed off practitioner of harmful hoodooery."

The first few minutes in the car, Teddy was fairly upbeat and chipper, explaining to Perry and Max about Heckle and Jeckle and how they need to aspire to the cartoon birds' levels of perceptions of human nature and intuitive intelligence if they were going to do their job well. In the weeks since staying with him, I had seen Perry and Max standing guard at the house or trailing me when I went out at least five different times. They had likely known Teddy longer than I had, yet he was talking to them like they had never met.

That he knew all of that, knew more about these men

than they probably knew about themselves, wasn't really in question. For all his foolishness and practiced assholery, my uncle was very clever and extremely perceptive. So he was either fucking with them because he was bored and wanted to irritate me, or he was putting off answering the question I had asked as soon as we had gotten into the car. I gave him a couple more minutes of extolling the virtues of cartoons as morality tales before I interrupted.

"No seriously. What is The Hungry Blade?"

He turned back around in his seat, his face falling into a more serious expression. "Yes, we need to talk about it before we get there. Might as well get it out of the way. Have you ever heard of a passion play?"

I glanced over at him. "You mean like the Mel Gibson Jesus movie?"

He rolled his eyes. "Yes, I suppose. The idea of a passion play is not that different than what The Hungry Blade originated from. Much like passion plays attempt to detail the last days of Jesus' life, the basis for The Hungry Blade was originally an attempt to detail Lucifer's fall from Heaven and the formation of infernal Hell."

I raised my hand to stop him. "Okay. A couple of questions. First, it sounds like you're saying the evil movie Marshall saw was based on something else. Second, you're making a point of saying 'infernal' Hell. Is that because its not run by the demons any more since the Hunter took over?"

He looked at me sourly. "I was getting to all that, and now you've ruined the dramatic tension I was building, but I guess it's better for you to ask questions as they come to you. I forget how new you are to all this. Okay, so I make the distinction of infernal Hell for two reasons. The first you've already guessed, which is that our buddy the Hunter has taken it over now, and as you saw during your time there, the demons that are left don't have the best time of it, even by Hell standards."

****

The second reason is that Hell existed, kind of, before Lucifer and his angels were sent there. You have to understand, you can't really apply concepts like time and space to places like Hell. There are some things that have always existed, and that includes the Seven Realms, of which Hell is one. But there was a long time before the war in Heaven happened, before Lucifer and his crew were cast out, that Hell was something different. It was controlled by and full of something else.

No, I don't know what. Not really. But it's said that when Lucifer was falling, whatever had occupied Hell before was pushed further out. Outside the Seven Realms and further away from our world and others like it. Maybe it's bullshit, but I've seen and learned enough to think it's not. Anyway, that's a story for another day. Today the story is about Lucifer and His Version of Hell: The Movie.

But as you so astutely interrupted, it didn't start out as a movie. It actually began as an ancient play of sorts. The only known copy of it was found in 1882 by British soldiers during their occupation of India. Supposedly it was pried out of the hands of some Calcutta death cult they were clearing out, and while the soldiers had no idea what it said, they knew it looked old enough and important enough to steal.

It made its way back to Europe, where it was examined and studied by several "experts" on the black market. It was written in Tamil, one of the oldest written languages in the world, and it was estimated to be nearly 4,000 years old. It didn't take long for one of the wealthier occult groups to scoop it up. After several years of study, they asked one of their members for help. He was heavily involved in the developing field of motion picture technology, and they wanted the manuscript turned into a movie.

I don't know the person's name, but I assume he was German, given the film's name. *Die hungrige Klinge*, or "The Hungry Blade", was made around 1888. It was only about ten minutes long back then, and while it was cutting edge at the time, it was very limited. There was no sound, and the sparse narration and dialog were on cards scattered between scenes of the movie. There were a few unique features about the film, however.

First, the director had taken the time to film each page of the original Tamil manuscript and splice those images into the movie. Just a frame here and there, so you'd never notice unless you slowed it down. Second, according to most accounts, the first time it was shown to the occultists that had the manuscript, a handful of them immediately went violently insane and a couple more started changing into...something not fun...within a week or two. This was an exciting development for those that weren't dead by the end of the month, because it meant the film had real power that transcended even the original document.

You have to bear in mind that these people...these kinds of people...they're not risk-adverse. The worse something is, the more dangerous it appears to be, the more they want it. They always assume they can control it, leverage it, hold it over someone's head. They think that just because they aren't dead yet, or in Hell yet, or whatever, that they're somehow special. Smarter and better than the rest.

So they waited a few weeks, then watched it again. This time, a few more went crazy or transformed, and the survivors convinced themselves they were not only safe, but were gaining new and powerful insights into the hidden worlds they wanted to tap into and ultimately master. Some of that was understandable, because they realized on the second viewing that the movie was changing too. It was longer and had new scenes, including some that incorporated their old, departed cult friends. But it also showed more of Hell, and to these people, any shred of forbidden knowledge is power. Unfortunately for them, it was almost like they were getting old radio signals from the moon or seeing light from a star that burned out a million years ago.

Because bear in mind, this is a group of overfed European nobility and merchants that are infernal occultists — or devil worshippers if you prefer the term — at a time when Lucifer has already been dead for hundreds of years by our world's clock. These fat fucks just didn't get the memo.

So on they go. The third viewing cuts the remaining number from twelve members down to five, one of which is the original director. The movie is now almost an hour long and is clearly growing more powerful with every viewing. The ones that are left, while not transforming into monsters per se, become even more evil and twisted than they were before and find it harder and harder to think about anything other than the film.

Whether the movie made them stop there or they decided to quit pushing their luck, I don't know. But apparently they took a break from showing it for a few years to build back up their numbers. And when they decided to show it again, they went public with it.

On July 10, 1893, there was a massive fire at the World's Fair in Chicago. Officially, sixteen people died in it, and it immediately became national news at the time. Unofficially, over fifty people died and another twenty were permanently institutionalized. That was the first public showing of the film.

Since then, the group has grown and shrank over the years, always keeping to the shadows. I think the risk of exposure at the fair incident scared them a bit, and the rumor is that now they only show the movie once a year. Only members of their group are allowed to watch it except for a single outsider—usually a lone projectionist or usher—who they leave alive to carry the tale out into the world.

Because they don't really want the movie to be a total secret, of course. They want it to be a legend. Gossip among those looking for something "extreme" or "really fucked up" will eventually lead some to track down the group. They'll think they've cracked the case, beaten the mystery, found a door into a secret world. And they'll demand their reward, to see the movie the following year.

And they'll get to see it, of course, in whatever form it might be at that time. And they'll die or go crazy. Or they won't--until the next year or three years after that. Because aside from the film's caretakers—who may or may not be those original surviving members, depending on who you believe—everyone goes in the end. Movie's gotta eat and all that.

So that's what I know about "The Hungry Blade". That's why I say this kid we're going to see is totally fucked.

****

I was gripping the steering wheel tightly, my stomach churning. For all that I'd seen since first entering my uncle's life, I realized this was the first time I was knowingly heading toward danger. In everything up to this point, I was just trying to do what I thought was best to survive. But this…I could tell Teddy was spooked, and he had lost any sense of humor about Marshall Abner's fate when he mentioned it this time around. For the first time in awhile, I found myself questioning what I was doing all this for. Was I really any different than the idiots intentionally watching that movie?

When I turned to look at him, I saw that Uncle Teddy was studying me. He gave me a thin smile and nodded.

"That worry you have now? Those misgivings? That's called common sense. This is a dangerous world you're in now, and while I can try to keep you safe from my enemies, if we're going to go chase down things like this, you need to know how bad it can get. I can't promise we'll win against the people I know, much less something like this. So if you want out, I get it. Drop me off and I'll have another car come pick me up to go talk to the Abner boy." His face looked tired and worried, and he wouldn't meet my eyes. I knew he was being sincere, but I could also tell he was scared to go by himself.

"Why don't we both just go home then? Why risk it, especially if he's a lost cause?"

He shook his head. "I've spent too long helping evil in this world. Turning a blind eye is no better. This is the first new information I've heard about the movie in years, and if I can stop it, I'm going to." He looked back at me. "But you aren't like me. You're a good person. There's no reason for you to get drug into my bullshit quest for redemption."

I tried to smile. "I'm a little freaked out yeah, but I'm not going anywhere. If you needed my help before, I know you need it against a spoopy movie like this."

Uncle Teddy quickly brightened. "You raise a good point, Cora. Like they say, spoopiness loves company."

****

It took five tries knocking at Marshall Abner's door before he answered it, and even though he was largely covered in multiple blankets, the smell of putrescent decay hit me hard enough that I had to fight hard to swallow back the bile rising in my throat. Marshall had a small oval slit uncovered that showed his eyes and nose, and even from that glimpse, it was clear he was very sick or dying. He stared blankly ahead, and when Teddy introduced us, he just shuffled back out of the way as a form of silent invitation.

The apartment we entered was drastically different than the building it was in. The outer hall was well-lit and clean, with fresh paint and nice carpet. The interior of Marshall's apartment looked much like Marshall himself—with one foot into Hell and the other on a banana peel.

He had followed us into the living room before lurching past to sit down in a recliner that looked to be half-consumed by something akin to black mold. Before his body and blankets obscured it, I thought I saw things moving on the surface of the stained chair. There was no way I was sitting down in there.

Teddy was snapping his fingers with a loud crack. "Mr. Abner…Marshall…I know this is hard for you. I know it's hard to focus. But can you talk to us? Can you tell us more about what you saw or might know? Any detail would be…"

The blankets fell away as the sound started—a soft, insidious song that seemed to be boring into the center of me. Marshall's face was all that was left of the old him apparently, as the rest was a fleshy ruin filled with sores and strange limbs that flailed around in various stages of decay. I tried to scream, and one of those limbs shot forward into my mouth, burning my tongue with an acrid film that seemed to coat its skin.

My last memory before everything changed was that the Marshall-thing seemed to be falling apart as the song emanated from it, as though the vibration of it was tearing him apart atom by atom. I watched him fall into a bloody disarray that matched the chaos in my head and the black static in my heart.

Then I was in a theater. I remember only a few seconds of it, but I recognized the place. It was a theater in my hometown, the Picture Palace. I remember thinking that was impossible because it had gotten torn down when I was a teenager, but then the screen lit up and I saw the movie was starting.

****

"Wake up, Cora. God, wake up, please."

I opened my eyes to Uncle Teddy's worried face looming over me. In the distance I could see the dark blue of the evening sky behind the imposing figures of Heckle and Jeckle. Confusedly, I sat up a little and looked around. We were on the sidewalk outside of Marshall's apartment. My eyes went wide as I remembered what had happened.

"Did you see that? Did Marshall..."

Teddy took the air out of me with a tight hug. When he pulled back, he was smiling coldly. "Turn out to be a weird hellbeast with no sense of personal boundaries? Yes. Did you see a theater too?"

I nodded again, my stomach going cold. "I think somehow he...it...it showed me the movie. In my head. I don't remember much, but I think that's what happened."

His expression turned hard. "I think you're right. I'm starting to wonder if this whole thing wasn't a trap for us from the start, but either way, it doesn't change anything."

"But what're we going to do?" I could hear my voice shaking, but I didn't care. "Are we going to turn into things like he was? I can't let that happen...I can't listen to that song again..."

Teddy froze as he stared at me. "Song? What song?"

"The song that was coming from him. The thing that tore him apart." I gave a shudder. "Please, I don't want to think about it anymore."

He hugged me again briefly and nodded. "I understand. We'll deal with that later. For now, let's take care of the movie."

I stood up slowly, my legs feeling wobbly but good enough to stay upright. "How are we going to take care of it?"

He grinned, his eyes glittering darkly at me. "We're going to find it and destroy it, along with any dumb motherfucker that gets in our way."

The Spoopiest Picture Show

"Do you remember your line?" Uncle Teddy cocked an eyebrow at me with the acerbic manner of a beleaguered stage director. "Do you?"

I grimaced at him as I scratched at my neck. "I do. It doesn't make sense, both as a 'line' and in the context of what we are about to do, but yes."

He squinted at me momentarily before letting out a sigh. "I keep hoping that you're joking when you say things like that, but then I see you're not and become sad. See that's the problem with you kids today. It's all farts and vaginas with you lot. No subtlety or style. And when it comes to chewing ass and kicking bubblegum? Why use planning or put a small effort into theatricality when you can just go in and shoot somebody?"

Shifting uncomfortably, I poked him in the arm. "Speaking of which, do you actually have a plan? Because all I've heard so far is a lot of vague lectures with seemingly no point aside from how awesome you are."

Snorting, he looked back across the street to the Rajah theater. It was probably a charming little place when its big signs were lit up and twinkling, but in the darkness of more than an hour past midnight, it sat in its spot on the street like a sullen giant frog waiting to swallow up any flies that dared get too close. I knew we had to do this, but I didn't know how we were going to do it. I mean that both from a "likelihood of success" standpoint and a "what's the fucking plan" standpoint. Teddy's silence did little to improve my estimation of the one or my understanding of the other.

"Can I at least take the devil coin off?"

He snapped his head around with a frown and look of concern. "Absolutely not. Just because we're about to take these fuckers down is no reason to risk it. You can deal with a little rash. Besides, there might be multiple reasons for your wearing it." His voice took on a mysterious tone and seemingly satisfied with my long-suffering eye roll, he turned back to watching the theater.

The "devil coin" was actually called a tumerin, and according to Teddy it had been the currency in Hell during Lucifer's reign. He said that it was now mainly used by ousted demons, infernal loyalists, and some dark occultists as a kind of black market capital and as a quick way to prove one's legitimacy in certain circles. Of course, that also meant that tumerin counterfeiting was rampant.

The way you could always tell a genuine coin of Hell was that it wouldn't burn or melt, no matter how hot the flame, and they always were imbued with a bit of infernal magic. Less than thirty minutes after I woke up on the sidewalk outside of Marshall Abner's apartment, Teddy was already stringing one of the coins around my neck. He said he couldn't cure the film's effects, but he could stop most of them temporarily — so long as I kept the coin on. When I asked why he hadn't made us fancy devil necklaces before we went into the doomed boy's apartment, he looked at me with disappointment, as though the answer was obvious.

"This isn't mosquito spray, Cora. You don't dabble with artifacts of Hell lightly. Or did you never see any of the *Hellraiser* movies?" When I had said I never had, he looked more horrified than...well, no, he literally looked more horrified than I've ever seen him. He held up his hand as he retrieved his phone and made a voice memo. Something along the lines of "Teach the girl about Pinhead". After a glance at me he sulkily added, "Find cursed movie and destroy it first so she can properly enjoy *Hellraiser*."

****

The two weeks between then and now had been somewhat miserable, but to Uncle Teddy's credit, he had found where the movie was going to be shown this year with amazing speed. I know he spent a couple of nights in his workshop making new dolls, so I suspect I know what he traded for the information, and more recently he disappeared one night for several hours. But whatever his methods, we were definitely in the right spot, as we had watched the sinister-looking caretakers escort the film in promptly at midnight. Just a few minutes later, several dozen people appeared from the shadows, both singly and in groups, and entered the Rajah as well. Soon all the bad people and one unwitting victim were inside.

When we had set up across the street a few minutes before midnight, I had asked Teddy what was going to happen to the poor guy or girl that worked at the theater? Shouldn't we try to warn them or save them? I knew the answer, of course, but it was still hard to swallow, and having him confirm it somehow made the burden easier to bear.

His voice was surprisingly soft when he spoke, though his face was stony in the dim light of the street. "You know we can't. They'll likely die or wind up like Marshall, but that can't be helped." He paused a moment before gripping my arm firmly with surprising strength. "You need to remember something in all this, Cora. We aren't heroes. We aren't trying to help the innocent. Our only two goals are to stop the bad things and stay alive. If some poor schmuck gets ground up as collateral damage, that's a shame, but better them than us."

I tried to tug my arm away and found I couldn't. "I get it, but I don't agree. We don't have to be selfish assholes about it. I understand why we can't warn anybody about this before it starts...I do. But if we can help someone once we're in there, why shouldn't we?" I yanked again and pulled my arm loose. "Why not try?"

Uncle Teddy gave a dry laugh. "You've been through a lot, and you've done really well. I wouldn't have you involved in my new work if I didn't think you were up to it. But you need to let go of the participation trophy, it's the thought that counts, trying your best is good enough bullshit that you've been force-fed for most of your life. That's feed for cattle. We are not cattle."

He pointed across at where several black robed figures were getting out of a dark SUV. "Those demonic fucks are not a teacher or boss or the IRS or pick your mundane authority figure that cattle seek to placate so they can keep eating and shitting in moronic peace. These things will quite literally rip us apart if we don't get this right, and that is far from the worst thing they can do to us."

He turned back to me. "And to be clear, that's not just for tonight. It's this life. We will do the best we can, but we always prioritize ourselves and our goal before anything else. Because not to sound like a conceited shit, but it actually matters if one or both of us dies. If we get cut down trying to help out some goober whose skillset consists of trying to not pick his pimples while he's refilling the popcorn popper, I don't think he's going to exactly pick up our mantle."

I smirked at him. "I guess by that logic, it matters a lot more if you die than me then."

He gave a look of surprise. "Well, yeah. Was that ever a question?"

****

When we left the car, I asked for the tenth time why we weren't bringing the guards. Wouldn't it be well-advised to have some muscle while we're dealing with crazed devil worshippers and monster-type things? Teddy shook his head and kept walking.

"No, they need to stay in the car."

In the days leading up to movie night, I had tried every way I could think of to get Teddy to tell me his plan. I knew he had one, and I knew he enjoyed torturing me with not knowing. It may be that he also had a legitimate reason for keeping me in the dark, but it didn't make me like it any better.

When I had asked about bringing weapons, he said there was no need and no point. If it came down to us having to physically fight all these people, even waiting as we were until many were hopefully dead from the night's partial viewing and ensuing chaos, we would lose. Which is when I brought up using guards again, which only earned me a small, smiling shake of the head.

So instead, I walked into the movie theater with my cell phone in one pocket and the car keys in the other. Unless someone wanted to take a selfie with me, I was kind of screwed. I trusted Teddy, but I'd be lying if I said I wouldn't have felt better if Heckle and Jeckle…fuck, Perry and Max were with us.

The lobby of the theater was empty, but it was far from quiet. Even through the sound dampening walls you could hear the screams and howls coming from the theater behind the concession stand. Putting a finger to his lips like a cartoon villain, Teddy crept over to the first of two large double doors that led into what was no doubt a blood bath by this point. With the fanfare of a self-satisfied mime or stage magician, he pulled out four thick zip ties and secured two around the handles of both sets of doors. When he eased back closer to me, I leaned in and whispered to him.

"Do you honestly think that's going to hold them?"

He gave me a knowing look. "Long enough, yeah."

I narrowed my eyes. "What about the emergency exits, smarty?"

Uncle Teddy held a hand up to his mouth in mock horror. "Oh no. Not the emergency exits. I guess I should have had them welded shut last night…oh wait, I did. If you're done embarrassing yourself, let's get to the projectors."

Grumbling into his back, I followed him around the corner and through a door marked "Staff Only". We had just started up the narrow set of stairs to the projection room when I heard a girl screaming up there. When we opened the door at the top, I saw why.

Three black robes lay puddled on the floor of the room near the door, and at first I thought their occupants were just gone. But then I saw the girl. It was hard to get my brain to reconcile what I was looking at, but she looked as though she was wrapped up in some kind of fleshy cocoon or meat anthill. Her body was wholly subsumed in a mass of rotten, writhing flesh that reminded me of what Marshall had looked like under his blanket. Except for her face, of course. Her face was held fast and pointed outward toward the images unfolding on the movie screen, and it was clear from her eyes that she was already well past the point of madness.

Teddy stepped forward, making a point of keeping me behind him. "Hello, fellow patrons of the arts. If you'll kindly untangle from the girl, we have some business to discuss."

I felt the urge to vomit as the things unspooled from around the young woman and let her collapse to the floor. Their movements reminded me of timelapses of growing mold as they slid apart and back into their robes. In a matter of seconds, there were three dark figures standing before us.

One of them stepped forward, the stench of decay wafting towards us at his approach. "So you still live. Interesting, but ultimately unimportant. Did you come here to watch the movie again, or simply to die?"

Teddy shook his head. "Neither one, Mr. Ringwraith. I came to find out who set us up. Who made that boy from last year into a booby trap for me. I would say it was one of my occultist frenemies, but that situation didn't come up until recently, and I get the idea that poor Mr. Abner had been cooking a lot longer than that."

Mr. Ringwraith let out a wet, mucousy laugh. "You know so little. I have no idea why they wanted to waste the effort on you. But no matter." It turned to the other two. "Kill them so we can get back to enuring the girl."

Teddy stepped back, in the process pushing me out of the doorway and into the small stairwell. "Hey, Mr. Ringwraith. You know who my favorite Tolkien character is? No, it's not the creepy old dude that likes to hang out with the hobbits all the time. It's Golem."

After a moment he looked at me expectantly and gave a theatrical cough. Glaring at him, I said my line with as little enthusiasm as I could muster. "It's pronounced Gollum."

Tapping me on the nose, Uncle Teddy grinned and turned back to the three robed monsters that were pressed against some invisible barrier at the edge of the projection room. "Oh yeah. I must have been thinking about something else."

There was a tremendous crash in the theater below, and the screams and wails took on a different quality that quickly dissolved into new hot, wet sounds. Mr. Ringwraith glanced out at the theater and then back at the invisible line he apparently couldn't cross. When he spoke, his voice was so thick with hatred and anger I had to fight keep my ground.

"What have you done?"

Uncle Teddy's smile had turned hard and nasty. "Which part? The part where I put a binding circle in the ceiling of this room so your dumb asses would be trapped in there or the part where my golems are mashing your little film club down there into a fine paste?"

"Impossible." The other two hooded creatures were at the window, but they were no more able to escape that way than through the door. "You cannot hold us forever, and then you will suffer for all time."

Teddy turned to me. "Shit, Cora. Did you hear that? We're going to suffer for all time." He took a step back. "Although he is right about one thing. That thing won't hold them forever."

My eyes widened. "Well then shouldn't we be leaving? Setting fire to the film or something?" Just then I saw Heckle and Jeckle appear at the bottom of the steps. They were naked and had a few chunks missing, but they climbed the steps nimbly enough. As they got closer, I saw they were smooth as dolls between their…

"Wait. Did you make them?" I had to shout the question, as they had entered the projection room now and were in the process of ripping the three ringwraiths apart like they were cotton candy.

Teddy nodded. "Yep. A golem is really just another kind of doll, you know. It takes some different parts and know-how, but I figured it out eventually. The key is using a live bird as the core." He gestured to an open place on Jeckle's back. I could just make out the edge of an iron cage, and beyond the bars, the flutter of black wings. "I find that magpies work best. They really are mean bastards."

He pointed to the tumerin necklace around my neck. "Which is the other reason for these. I have good control over these two, but with this much killing, they're apt to get into a bloodlust." He winced as Heckle started stomping the theater girl curled into a fetal position near the projector. "Ugh. Case in point. These coins are specially spelled so they can still distinguish the two of us while they're in berserker mode. The movie won't burn, but they can rip it up enough that it'll be safe to carry until we can properly dispose of it."

I was a bit amazed, but irritated as well. "You could have let me in on all this, you know. So I didn't have to be terrified the whole night. I could have helped more than provide set-up for a lame punchline."

Uncle Teddy snickered. "It was better this way. These people…often some of them are sensitive, even fully psychic. Until you have more experience and control, it can be a risk for you to know too much ahead of time. Plus, this is your first time doing this sort of thing by choice instead of necessity. Most people can't walk into this kind of horror knowingly, especially without feeling assured they'll come out of it okay. Now I know you can." His smile soured as he began to look crestfallen. "And it wasn't a lame punch…"

"The Blind Court." Mr. Ringwraith's voice was coming from between the fingers of Heckle's massive hands as he prepared to crush the last bit of sentient hellflesh in the room.

Teddy's face visibly paled as he quickly turned toward the voice. "You're a fucking liar."

A small laugh oozed out of the golem's fist. "You should have let the movie have you. It would have been a mercy compared to what they will…" Its words were cut off as Heckle squeezed tighter, sending streams of black ichor out onto the floor.

I touched Teddy's arm. "What is it? What was he talking about? What's the Blind Court?"

He tried to smile but his eyes were far away. "Nothing, Cora. It was just a nasty hellthing wanting to worry us. It's nothing." He refocused on the golems in the room. "Rip the film to shreds and put it in the box we brought. Wash off and put your clothes back on before you come outside. No need to cause a scene. We'll pick you up in an hour." He glanced my way, but didn't meet my eyes. "Let's go, my sweet niece. They can finish up here with a nice fire while we go get pancakes. Don't you want pancakes?"

He was already halfway down the stairs and I could hear the stress in his voice. The fear. We might be safe for the moment, but it didn't feel that way. Rubbing my neck where the coin touched, I again found myself weighing how deeply I wanted to get involved in this world, this life. There was no question it was an ugly, terrifying place to be, but did I want to leave Teddy to face it alone?

He turned back as he reached the car, his eyes sad but knowing. He always could tell what I was thinking. "Or if you don't want pancakes, you can just head out and I can get some on my own. You need to start spending your twenty million some time, after all."

I raised an eyebrow. "I thought it was ten million."

He shrugged. "Combat pay."

Smiling, I gave him a quick hug as I reached the car. "Nah, I'm good where I am. And I really do want some pancakes."

Uncle Teddy's smile was genuine this time. A few minutes later we were in an all-night diner laughing and chowing down as we heard fire trucks rushing by. I knew he was keeping things from me, but I would give him some time before I pressed the issue. For the time being, being alive and in that diner with him was enough. There was nowhere I'd rather be.

Between the Rows

"This is really lame."

I shot Alison an irritated look. She seemed to ignore it as she stared past me at the signs plastered around the ticket booth for the Jefferson Farm Corn Maze. My sister was always a naysayer when it came to stuff like this, but her comment was still tactless, even for her. It was Jenny's idea after all — the first suggestion or sign of enthusiasm she had shown since she'd come to live with us a month earlier. If Alison kept shitting on her idea, she might retreat back into her shell for good this time.

Turning to Jenny, I smiled. "You have to forgive Alison. She was born with a handicap, you understand. It's called being a fucking bitch." Jenny's eyes twinkled with surprise and merriment as she looked up at me, and she let out a light laugh when Alison punched me in the arm.

"No, I get it." Jenny said more seriously. "It might be kind of lame. But it looked fun on the internet, and I thought we could have a good time. Get into the Halloween spirit a bit."

Alison interrupted her. "You're right. It'll probably be fun." She looked around with a sigh. "Sorry, not trying to be a downer. Tell you what. You two get our tickets and I'll get us drinks."

I followed her gaze and saw a large food truck set up serving soft drinks and beers while another nearby truck sold funnel cakes and popcorn. She was eyeing the guy selling beers with interest, and I had to concede that he looked just greasy enough to be her type. Shrugging, I gave her a nod and turned with Jenny toward the ticket line.

I had never known our cousin Jenny very well. She was

the only child of our mother's brother, and they lived on the other side of the state from us, though it wasn't so far a distance that it explained how rarely we saw them. The truth was that her family had always been fairly isolated. They would come around at Christmastime or Thanksgiving maybe once every three or four years, but even then they didn't talk a lot or stay very long.

They were never rude or weird-acting, just kind of quiet. Uncomfortable-looking or like they felt kind of out of the loop because they weren't around more. I'd felt a bit sorry for them growing up, but I still always enjoyed their visits because of Jenny.

Jenny was a lot more outgoing than her parents, and even though she was a girl, I always clicked with her a lot more than Alison did. Maybe it was because Alison was older—she was worried about what she was going to do when she graduated college next spring while me and Jenny were just getting into our last year of high school—or maybe it was just that their personalities didn't mesh well. Either way, over the years I had been guilty more than once of wishing that I could swap out Alison for Jenny on a permanent basis.

Jenny poked me in the side. "Do you want to do any of the other stuff, or just the main corn maze?" We were getting close to the front of the line, and her question prompted me to look at the menu of options hanging above the ticket booth window. There was the corn maze, a smaller "haunted" corn maze, and a hay ride.

I weighed the money as well as Alison's patience in my head. "Hmm. It's already past nine and the corn maze looks huge. You cool with just doing that? I imagine it'll take awhile." I left off the rest of my thought, that Jenny didn't need to be exposed to whatever fake blood and violence would be waiting for us on the haunted maze. She seemed to consider it for a moment before nodding.

"Yeah, that sounds good. I bet we'll be in the corn maze for a long time anyway."

****

The night we found out Jenny was coming to live with us was a Saturday just like this one. I had planned on staying in and watching t.v. that night, and Alison was home for the weekend to see some guy she was dating. Or at least one of the guys she was dating. While we hadn't talked about it directly, I had the distinct impression that she had a boyfriend at college too, and that most likely neither guy knew about the other. Not that I cared — if someone was dumb enough to date her in the first place, I had very little sympathy to spare.

I remember our parents coming home from shopping and being strangely quiet. They had called us into the kitchen, our mother looking like she was in shock, her eyes red but not teary, our father rubbing her back with one hand while distractedly pulling at his mustache with the other. After a few moments of tense silence, our father started to explain.

There had been some kind of incident at Jenny's house. A home invasion possibly, though no one could say for sure. All that was certain was that she had come home the night before from a football game to find that her parents were both gone and that there was blood all over the living room.

Our father had made a point of explaining that Jenny had two friends with her when she discovered they were gone, and that she had been at the football game for hours before that. As though we needed some reassurance that she wasn't the one who had hurt her own parents. I felt mildly irritated and offended by the suggestion. Jenny was one of the nicest and gentlest people I'd ever known, and even in my limited time with her over the years, I knew she loved her parents very much. The idea of her hurting them or somehow being tied into their disappearance…well, it was just absurd. Still, I pushed down my frustration at my father's delivery of the terrible news and tried to listen.

So far there was no sign of them. Their phones and cars, wallets and keys, all those things had been left behind. After a few hours of investigation, and child services determining she was going to have to be placed with a relative because she was still 17, our parents had gotten the call. Until her parents were found alive, however unlikely that may be, or she turned 18, she needed a place to stay, and we were her only relatives.

****

For not the first time, I felt a thrill of excitement at the idea of having Jenny around. I had always wanted to be closer with my big sister, but we were very different from each other, and as we had gotten older those differences seemed to multiply. I loved Alison, but I didn't think I liked her that much, and I certainly couldn't say we were very good friends.

Jenny, on the other hand, was awesome. We had similar interests, and she didn't respond to everything with sarcasm or like she was defending against some kind of attack. Just the opposite. She was calm and laid-back, with an enthusiasm and sweetness that made you feel better just being around her. By the time Alison got back with our drinks, I was over my earlier anger and back to having a good time. Alison seemed in a better mood too, leading us to the long line to get into the corn maze without any of her usual eye-rolling or complaints.

Jenny handed out small maps to each of us. Looking at the small square of paper, I saw with surprise it was a rough drawing of the corn maze itself. I held it up to Jenny. "Isn't this kind of cheating?"

She grinned. "Nah, not really. It helps some, but once you're in there, everything looks the same. I usually find the map messes me up more than it helps, but we've got it if we want to use it at least."

Alison was still studying it when she asked, "So you've done these mazes before?"

Jenny nodded. "Yeah, me and my…my family used to do them almost every year. A tradition I guess." Her expression grew sad for a moment before brightening again. "But the maze is different every year, even if you come back to the same place. The only advantage I have is some experience."

Alison raised an eyebrow at her. "Corn maze experience? Is that a thing?"

Our cousin grinned and gave a shrug as we moved up in the line. "It's more useful than you might think."

****

There were a surprising number of people at the Jefferson Farm Corn Maze—kids strung out on sugar running to get on the hay ride as they were chased by beleaguered parents, clusters of squealing teenagers running out of the haunted maze to the repetitive whining roar of a chainless chainsaw, and in our own line, a mixture of young and old waiting for their turn to enter the giant corn maze.

As far as we could tell, they were letting in groups of four or five people every couple of minutes. I guessed the idea was that you would get a fairly even number of people coming and going from the maze by staggering people's entry. While this may have worked wonders for the isolated ambiance inside the maze itself, on the outside it kind of sucked. We edged our way forward, but after over forty minutes we still hadn't made it to the front of the line. Jenny had actually made a supply run at the twenty-minute mark, bringing us back fresh drinks and funnel cake.

Then, when we were ten people from entering, a man who seemed to work there came up to the gatekeeper of the maze, telling him it was time to cut off the line for the night. The gatekeeper, a boy who looked only a couple of years older than me, cupped his hands around his mouth and yelled to the line of seventy or eighty people that the maze was going to have to be closed to new entries after three more groups. If someone was further back in the line than that, they could go to the ticket booth to get a new ticket for any other night in October.

I understood the logic—the maze had to close some time, after all—but I still found myself anxiously wondering if we would make the cut. I knew it meant a lot to Jenny, and the odds of wrangling Alison to come out a second time this month were slim to none. To my relief, the gatekeeper walked past us and cut off the line right behind where we were standing. A few of the people muttered as they shuffled off, but then we were being ushered into the maze as one big final group and the noises and lights of the outside world faded away between the rows of corn that surrounded us on every side.

The corn maze felt eerily separate from the place we had just left. The corn dampened sound and light, and with no lights set up within the maze itself, everything had a fuzzy blue-black quality to it. The half moon overhead and the ambient light from the rest of the attractions and booths provided just enough illumination to make out the dirt path as we walked forward, a faintly visible ribbon of dirt that wound and crisscrossed the further we went into the maze.

We had no flashlights, but instead took turns using our phones' flashlight setting to provide some additional light. In some ways it only made things more disorienting. The small circle of bright white light would make its best feeble effort to cut through the murk, but it also made the surrounding dark seem that much darker. After a few minutes, we gave up on using our lights unless we were checking the map for some sign of where we actually were.

The thing with a corn maze is that, like Jenny had said, everything looks the same. You're surrounded by twelve-foot high stalks on every side, so tightly planted that you can't see more than a foot into the rows, much less the path that is ten feet away on the other side. And the corn all looks the same. You try to find distinct curves or intersections — things that are unique enough that you can find their twin on the small map and get a bead on your location. Then you realize that the map is not entirely accurate and that there are several places on it that could be your special spot.

So do you pick one and try to use the map? You can, but that only works if you know where you're starting from. Do you ignore the map and just keep going? It's an option, but it's also a good way to wander for hours. We had been in there over thirty minutes with no real discernable progress toward the exit when Jenny asked a question.

"I wonder if you could stay in here after they're closed for the night?"

At first, I misunderstood what she meant. I thought she was worried we might get stuck in here overnight, and I was quick to assure her that we could always just push through the corn, or barring that, yell until someone found us, as they undoubtedly would have people checking for stragglers before calling it a night.

But Jenny shook her head. "No, I mean, if we wanted to stay after it was closed, just to explore and say we did it, could we get away with it?"

I'd expected Alison to have some smart comment at the suggestion, but she surprised me by showing interest. "You know, I bet we could. Even if they send people through to get out people that are lost or don't want to leave, they can't find everybody. Particularly if you don't want to be found. If we hid in the corn deep enough and stayed quiet, I bet they'd never know it. Then we could do what we wanted and leave when we get ready."

I hated to be the wet blanket, but the idea sounded really

boring and dumb to me. Plus, if I'm being honest, I'm not much for breaking the rules. Aside from any far-flung fears of the police being called if we were found lingering after hours or they noticed our car had never left the lot, just the embarrassment of being yelled at and escorted off the farm by the staff made my stomach squirm.

Still, I didn't want to appear uncool or unfun, so I tried to look casual as I shrugged. "Even if we could, what would be the point? We got in here after ten and it's close to eleven now. You have to figure that they're going to let people stay until at least eleven-thirty or twelve, right? Otherwise people would get pissed for not getting long in the maze. So we're talking about killing time for an hour or more, then hiding in the corn for what, another hour? Just so we can walk around the same maze we can just walk around now?" I saw Jenny's disappointed expression and tried to soften my words. "I mean…we can if you want, I just don't know that we'll have fun." I could hear the insincerity in my voice and hoped I was the only one.

"You suck. I bet you graduated first at the academy." Alison was frowning at me.

I raised an eyebrow. "Academy?"

She gave me a toothy smile. "The Fun Police Academy, you little bitch." She turned to Jenny. "Ignore him. He's all butthurt if he doesn't return a library book on time. Plus, he checks out library books. So his vote doesn't count. And if you're down, I'm down."

I felt anger and embarrassment tightening my chest, but I couldn't think of any reply that wouldn't make me look worse. Besides, Jenny was already nodding excitedly and looking back to me. "Are you cool with it, Kyle?"

I smiled weakly. "Yeah, sure. I'm probably wrong and it'll be really fun." However, I couldn't help but add, "And if we get bored, we can always change our minds."

We started back to walking through the maze, and occasionally I would see a glimpse of flashlight through the rows or hear someone talking or laughing some distance away, but we didn't run into anyone else despite the massive amount of people that had been let in before us. At eleven, an announcement went out over a hidden set of speakers somewhere.

The Corn Maze is now closed. Please exit the maze immediately. Thank you for coming. If you can't find your way out, yell and we will come find you.

Alison poked me in the ribs and waggled her eyebrows. "See, scaredy cat? Not so long a wait after all." Glancing back at Jenny she grinned. "Let's find a good hiding spot."

****

We walked for a couple of more minutes before finding a secluded corner that seemed to be especially dense with corn stalks. One concern was that if you went in deep on one side you may be visible on another side if a different part of the maze cut too close to your hiding spot. But it seemed we had made it to one of the outer edges of the map, and as we slowly threaded our way into the corn there were no signs of another path coming into view. Instead there was just increasing darkness and the claustrophobic feel of stalks pressing in on you from all sides as a dry, leafy smell filled your nose and coated your tongue.

Jenny was holding my hand as we went into the corn, and I felt sure she could tell my own was sweating. But she never said anything, and as we settled into a spot to wait out anyone searching the maze, she gave my hand a squeeze.

"Thank you for doing this, Kyle. It means a lot to me." I could barely make her out in the dark, but I smiled at her words anyway, squeezing her hand back.

"Sure thing. It's kind of cool." In truth, I could barely breathe in that place, my chest feeling like it was surrounded by a slowly tightening belt as the minutes crawled by. I checked my phone and saw that twenty minutes had passed. Speaking to where I thought Alison was next to me, I let out a dry croak. "We good? No sign of anyone."

"Yeah, let's get back out. Just be quiet though."

I started back the way we had come — the way I thought we had come, at least — but I didn't see any break in the corn ahead of us. If anything, it seemed to get darker. After a few more feet I knew why.

"There's a wall here."

"What?" Alison was coming up behind me and I could hear the irritation in her voice. "What the fuck do you mean, a wall?" She reached passed me and put her hand against the brick wall. I heard her let out a breath and suddenly her cellphone's light was on, illuminating a gray brick wall buried among the corn and going up at least ten feet. As she panned the light from side to side, we could see that the wall stretched on to our left and right as far as the light would reach. "What...I don't understand. We would have seen this, right? We would have seen a giant brick wall when we pulled into the parking lot."

"I think there's more corn on the other side." We both looked at Jenny as she spoke, her eyes wide. "That's the only thing that makes sense. They must have more corn growing outside the wall so from the ground it looks like it's just corn, when really the maze has walls on it." She bit her lip as she looked up at it. "I dunno. Maybe it's so they can control how people come and go? Keep people from sneaking in without paying, I guess?"

I nodded, trying to speak with a confidence I didn't feel. "Yeah, I bet that's it. It makes sense that they want to keep people out that don't pay for a ticket." And it did make a certain amount of sense, even if something in my core said it was a lie. "Either way, we know a direction that isn't blocked, so let's head that way and find our way out."

I didn't know if this last was true either, as I had thought we were heading in the right direction before when we had hit the wall. Still, I turned left and stayed with the wall for a few feet before veering away in a direction I hoped would lead us back to a path. This time it did, and I found myself taking in burning lungfuls of the cold night air once I wasn't surrounded by the corn any more. Jenny patted my back and I smiled at her.

"I'm okay, just glad to be out of the corn." Looking around, I frowned. "But I don't think I have any idea where we are."

Alison took the map from me and started alternating between studying it and looking at the path we were on, trying to discern some unique feature that would tell us what path this actually was. She stopped when the stillness of the night was pierced by the high-pitched squeal of a pig. We all looked at each other with anxious expressions. They called this place a farm but it was an attraction, not a real working farm with livestock. Why would there be a pig out here?

I was about to ask that very question when the music began. Strange, discordant music that would occasionally be punctuated by another cry from a pig or some other creature. And underneath it all, we could hear the low, throaty thrum of some kind of singing. I looked up at the inky sky as though it would help me place where the sounds were coming from. I couldn't tell much, but it was somewhere close by. Somewhere in the maze, if I had to guess.

Now I did speak, my voice barely a whisper and my own fear reflected in their faces as they looked at me. "We're not alone in here."

****

After a moment of conversation, we decided to head straight in the direction we thought would put us out somewhere between the entrance to the maze and the parking lot. We started moving, ignoring the path and just quietly pushing our way through the corn stalk walls of the maze while trying to stay oriented towards our goal. We were relying on our sense of direction and the brick wall to our right—our theory being that the wall was likely fairly straight and if we kept it on our right we shouldn't get turned around.

The music and pig cries didn't lessen as we moved. If anything they got louder, but I wasn't sure it was because we were moving closer to the source. It was almost like the air itself, or maybe the corn, was suffused with the sounds, and the longer we walked, the more I felt that the animal squeals were digging into my brain and the eerie rhythms of the music and singing were worming into my bones.

Then we hit another wall.

"Fuck!" Alison said in a loud whisper. She turned to me and I could see how upset she was getting. I wanted to hug her, but instead I tried to sound calm.

"It's okay. Let's turn left. The wall has to end because this is the side we entered on. There has to be a break somewhere, right?"

Alison and Jenny nodded and we went on. Between our intermittent walks through the deeper corn and my steadily rising panic, I was finding it harder and harder to breathe. Maybe that's why I didn't hear the footsteps behind us. I felt a hand close tightly on the back of my shirt as Alison whispered in my ear.

"There's someone behind us. I thought I heard them a minute ago, but I couldn't see anything. Then when we left that last patch of corn, I know I heard someone else move the stalks after we were all out." My heart leapt but I forced myself to keep walking. Jenny was holding my hand again, but she was on the opposite side of where Alison was talking, so I didn't know if she had heard what my sister had said.

I gave Jenny's hand a squeeze to get her attention and spoke in a slightly louder whisper than Alison's. "There's someone behind us. We need to run. Alison, hold my hand and we all stay together. When we see a break in the wall, we turn and head for the parking lot." Alison took my other hand as I strained my ears for sounds from behind us. I couldn't be sure, but I thought I could barely make out the rustle of a heavy foot stepping on one of the dead corn leaves that littered the floor of our current path.

Squeezing both of their hands, I whispered, "1...2...3...go!", and we took off running. Alison was faster than either myself or Jenny, but she slowed her pace as she realized she was going to pull too far ahead to hold my hand. I kept looking to my right, waiting for some sign of light or the world beyond the corn. But all I saw was darkness. It seemed impossible. The maze was big, but it wasn't that big. We were moving at a good rate of speed and had already been walking in this direction for several minutes before we broke into a run.

The sounds of music and animals had receded for a time, but they returned now and seemed to come from everywhere. I began looking in every direction, desperate for some sign of escape, some indication that we were finally out of the maze. Then I saw light ahead of us. Almost crying with relief, I surged ahead, pulling Alison and Jenny along with me.

****

We stumbled out into a large open circle somewhere deep within the maze. There were tall torches spaced around the perimeter, and in the center was a small group of people wearing robes and carved wooden masks. Some of them were singing while others played odd instruments, but as we broke through the corn two of them stopped and looked at us for a moment. I was so shocked by what I was seeing that it took me a moment to register that Jenny had pulled free of my hand and run to the staring couple.

When they removed their masks, I understood both more and less. It was Jenny's parents. She was hugging them and talking excitedly, though their conversation was in hushed tones that didn't carry to us over the sound of the music and singing. I heard a new squeal and realized that there were massive looming shadows back behind the people. Suddenly the music and singing stopped and the crowd parted for the shadows to step forward.

They were boars. Four massive black boars that all sported sharp, yellowed tusks that they swiped at the air as they trotted forward into the center of the clearing. Their eyes seemed to gleam red in the firelight, and I felt my bowels loosening as they stared at us with their small, evil glares. Not knowing what else to do, I looked at Jenny, who was absently patting one of the boars as she smiled up at her mother.

"Jenny? What is all this?"

She looked at me, her face hardening. "This is what's necessary, Kyle. I know you feel scared and betrayed, but we don't have a choice in this."

I shook my head, bewildered. "What? Who is we? What are you talking about?"

She sighed and gestured at the group of people gathered around them. "This is my real family. My parents and I are part of a very special group. I guess you could call it a religion, though that's not really right. But the patrons of our way of life…of our power and knowledge…they're losing a…" She smiled ruefully and shook her head as her mother patted her shoulder. "No, they've lost a battle against a stronger foe. There is a new king of Hell, and we must pledge our allegiance to him before it is too late."

One of the other people stepped forward and pulled off their mask, revealing the plump, dark-skinned face of a woman that looked like an elementary school teacher or librarian. "That is blasphemy! The infernal order will be restored! I have tried to hold my tongue, but we should not be throwing our lot in with that thing, even if it would let us."

Jenny's father gestured and one of the other masked figures punched the woman in the stomach hard enough that she doubled over onto the dirt. "Beatrice, I've told you before. You're either onboard or you're meat. Guess you've made your choice." He stroked Jenny's hair and in a softer tone, "Honey, it's time to prepare the vessels."

Jenny nodded and took up a large bowl that was sitting nearby on the ground. As if on cue, the boars all simultaneously knelt down as she began to dip her hand into the bowl and pull out a white paste of some kind. One by one, she painted symbols on the large, wide foreheads of the beasts as her mother intoned some kind of prayer.

"Great Hunter, new King of Hell, we beseech you to take this offering in your name. Take these creatures as your vessels, use them for your ends and make their hunt, your hunt. Their kills, your kills. And know by the blood and the fear and the life that is consumed that we pledge to serve you as we served the Infernal Court in times past. This we pledge."

With that, she turned and pointed at Beatrice. "You are not a part of this. You are now a part of them. The meat. The prey." As one, the boars turned and regarded her briefly with the same hatred they had previously reserved for Alison and me.

"You're all fucking crazy." Alison had let go of my hand and took a step forward before a warning snort from the closest boar made her retreat. She pointed her finger at Jenny. "You fucking bitch. We took you in. Kyle has done everything to make you feel better. And what, it's all a trick? A trap? Because you're all part of some satanic cult or some bullshit?"

Jenny smiled thinly at her and waggled her hand. "Eh, technically we're not satanic, but potato tomato. Pretty much, yeah. But you should be saving your breath. You know, for the running and screaming."

Alison stepped forward again and I saw she had a small can in her hand. Pepper spray. "Way ahead of you, cunt." She hit the button and quickly fanned it back and forth into the faces of the four boars. The maze echoed with their angry screams of pain as Alison spun back to me and grabbed my arm. "Go!"

We plunged back into the corn, my sister's speed and strength causing her to nearly drag me along as we went off in a new direction from the way we started. There was no time or breath to spare for talking or planning. I was just trying to not slow her down as my lungs burned and my heart thudded in my ears. Almost like the end of a terrible dream, I thought I could make out electric lights ahead. The ticket booth.

I never saw the thing that tripped me. One moment I was up, still running and keeping decent pace with Alison, and the next moment I was covered in dirt and gasping to reclaim the breath that had been knocked out of me. She stopped immediately and came back to pick me up. That was all the time the boars needed.

A black blur swept by and drove her off her feet. She landed ten feet further away, having actually skidded out of the edge of the corn and bumped against a trash can filled with the remains of that night's crowd. I crawled forward and got to my feet, intent on helping her, but as I moved past the last of the corn, two of the boars bore down on her again, impaling her leg and her side with their now-bloody tusks. I screamed and went to attack them, to stop them from hurting her more, when I heard Alison's voice.

"Go…run…now…take them…" I saw she was pointing with a twisted hand to where her pepper spray had fallen. It was attached to her car keys. I picked them up, planning on using the spray against the boars again, but a third was on her now too, all of them stomping and cutting and biting as they tore her apart. It was too late — or at least that's what I told myself as I looked on in terror.

So I ran. Tears streaming down my face, I passed the ticket booth and the gate before turning to head into the parking lot. The boars didn't follow, and though I could barely see through my sobbing, I managed to find the car easily in the mostly empty lot. I got in and was cranking up when I heard a knock at my window. I jumped and looked out to see Jenny smiling at me.

"We got our two sacrifices, so the boars aren't coming after you. I'm glad that Beatrice decided to pipe up. I didn't want you to be taken tonight." She looked slightly sad. "I really did always like you best, Kyle."

I didn't want to roll down the window, so I just yelled through the glass. "I'm going to fucking kill you." She said something else, but I was already slamming the car into reverse with the intention of running her over. I stopped to put it in drive, and when I looked up, she was gone.

****

I told my parents and the police what happened, but no evidence has been found. No suspects have been arrested. The cornfield has been abandoned and Jenny has joined her parents as missing persons. I know that no one believes me. At least not the more fantastic parts of what happened. My parents think they were part of some crazy cult, and that I either imagined or exaggerated the boars and the walls and the rest. I can't say I blame them. When they checked the cornfield, they didn't find any walls or signs of animals out there.

But I know what happened to me. What happened to my sister. And I know it's not over. Because I remember the last thing that Jenny said as I tried to run her down for killing Alison, for betraying all of us.

"See you next October."

The Unquiet Spirit of Amerson Park

I work as a home caregiver for a local agency in Kentucky. I'm not a nurse, though I have some basic training in CPR and First Aid, and I've gone through classes so I'm able to render some level of help to our clients that need physical assistance. For the most part though, my job is to check in on people, help them do chores they have difficulty doing on their own, like getting groceries or doing laundry, and drive them to appointments as needed.

The story I'm about to tell has been changed enough that I'm not violating client confidentiality, but I assure you that the core elements of it are true.

About three months ago, I started seeing a new client, Peter Phelps. When I reviewed his casefile, I learned that Peter was a 55 year-old man who lacked a right arm due to a birth defect. This wasn't the reason for his home care, but rather that he was in the last stages of liver failure due to chronic alcoholism. His physical condition was deteriorating fast, and my supervisor told me that he was probably a "stop-gap client", which was what they called it when we were only providing services until home nursing or hospice started up. In Peter's case, he already had a nurse checking in on him twice a week, and my job was primarily to get him groceries, prepare meals, and do some light cleaning the three days a week I visited him.

I liked Peter from the first time I met him. He had a dry sense of humor, and while there was a sadness that lingered about him most of the time, he seemed very kind too. We would chat as I folded towels or swept the floor, and by the second week I found myself sometimes staying a few minutes over my time just to finish whatever we were talking about.

He seemed more interested in hearing stories from me than telling them, and I noticed that when he did tell me something, it was almost always from someone else's life rather than his own. I've done this job long enough to know that some people are very private or aren't comfortable talking about themselves, particularly with people they barely know. So I didn't find it all that strange that I knew very little about Peter's past even though I'd spent hours talking to him.

What did surprise me was the question he asked one afternoon as I was finishing up a round of dusting. "Do you want to know what happened to my arm?" He gestured to the empty space at his right shoulder, and while I knew what he meant, I didn't know why he was asking. I tried to keep my tone light as I responded.

"I think I remember reading in your file that you were born without it, right?" I felt uncomfortable, and I was worried about hurting his feelings or saying the wrong thing about something I thought might be a sensitive subject. He was quiet for a moment and I began to think the conversation might be over, but then I saw him shake his head out of the corner of my eye.

"No…No, I know that's what they say. What your file says, what everything says, but that's not so. It's going to sound crazy, but if you want to hear about it, I'll tell you. If not, we can talk about something else." I turned to look at him and he was smiling. I believed him that he would be fine either way, but I could also see that he hoped I'd say yes. He wanted to talk to somebody about whatever weirdness this was. So against my better judgment, I told him to tell me what really happened to his missing right arm.

****

I know going into this that you probably won't believe me. That's okay. I got used to people not believing me when I was a kid. After a few arguments with my family and a few trips to a shrink, I learned to keep my lips zipped on that topic most of the time. As an adult, you're only the second person I've ever tried to tell this story.

The first was this girl I was dating when I was…what? Twenty-five? Her name was Abigail. She was a beautiful girl inside and out, and there was a time when I thought she was the one for me. Wanted to marry her, the whole nine yards. Then I made the mistake of confiding in her. Telling her what I'm about to tell you.

Have you ever watched someone fall out of love with you? I mean actually seen that light, that living thing that was in their eyes when they looked at you, just wither and die? I hope not. You're young, but I hope you never do. I saw it when I was telling her this story, and it's—as you'd guess—a pretty terrible thing to see.

It wasn't until much later that I realized I had done both me and Abigail a service in telling her my secret. She loved me, sure, but not that much. Enough to listen, enough to not laugh. Enough to wait another month before she found some other reason that we needed time apart. To spare me the embarrassment of her telling me she wasn't going to be stuck with some lunatic that thought a monster took his arm.

I'm sorry, I'm getting off-topic. The point is, I'm past worrying about what people think. Maybe I am crazy after all. But crazy or not, I have enough sense to know I'll likely be dead in six months, and you may be one of the last friendly faces I ever run across. And I don't need you to believe me. I just need you to listen and not make fun of me.

Okay? Good.

When I was twelve years old, I lived with my parents in

a small town called Westerfield. It's about three hours east of here, and I doubt you've ever been or even heard of it. For the most part, Westerfield is a normal, mediocre small town. Back then we had a two-theater movie theater, a few chain restaurants, and more than our share of farms around, but not much in the way of fun for boys looking for a good time without getting into bad trouble.

I had been friends with Jack Paulson and Steve Marks since third-grade, and we really weren't bad kids. We would occasionally throw rocks at the trains as they passed through town or trespass on a dare, but nothing like some of the boys we knew. We never hurt anything or anybody — we were just bored.

That's part of what always made Halloween such a great time for us. We were getting older, and we knew our time for trick-or-treating was getting close to an end. And we still liked candy, but it wasn't like we couldn't get it any other way. I think that the reason we loved Halloween so much was because it gave us a way of holding on to being a kid a bit longer. Something to be excited for, to look forward to.

And if part of that was the trick or treating, part of it was us trying to tell each other scary stories, both as entertainment and in an attempt to freak each other out. It never really worked — we knew the stories weren't real, and if I'm being honest, we did a fairly bad job of telling them in the first place. But none of that stopped us. Every year, without fail, we would circulate several stories of how a dead body was found over at this abandoned house (and it might have moved) or how so and so's aunt had once seen a ghost levitate her living room table. Silly shit for the most part.

Then Jack told us about the thing in Amerson Park.

He had heard about it from his brother, who was older and in the military. A few days earlier, the brother had been home on leave and was talking to Jack about different places he and his friends hung out at — meaning me and Steve, though Jack's brother didn't know our names. He told Jack to stay away from Amerson Park, especially at night. That there was a strange homeless man that lived there, and Jack's brother had heard he was dangerous. By itself, that might have kept us away. But then his brother had added that, according to some people, the man wasn't really alive and was haunting the place. Whatever Jack's brother's intention, his warning immediately made Amerson Park the most intriguing place in town to us.

The park was small and rarely used, tucked away in an older part of town that was full of closed stores and ramshackle houses. As far as I knew, I had only been to the park once, and it was with my parents when I was younger. There was a small creek that ran through the property, covered at one point by a wooden bridge that had probably once been charming, but now looked like it was held together by termites and mold. The outing with my parents had ended when my father realized it didn't live up to memories from his own youth, and me and my friends had never had a reason to go so far outside of our normal stomping grounds to visit. Until now, that was.

The plan was simple. We were allowed to go out trick-or-treating by ourselves between 6 and 8 pm. So long as we stuck together, didn't eat any candy until we got home and it was checked, and weren't out past 8, we were cool. We figured it would be about a thirty-minute fast walk outside of our normal trick-or-treat circuit to get to the park and another thirty to get back. Allowing time to explore, we should still have a good thirty minutes for trick-or-treating after we were back closer to our neighborhood.

The only real point of contention was the last. Did we trick-or-treat before or after? Jack and I wanted to do the park first, while Steve wanted to prioritize candy. Steve's eyes had been big as dinner plates when Jack had told us about the man in the park, so I suspected he was hoping to distract us long enough with trick-or-treating that we abandoned the park idea altogether. But majority ruled, and to the park we went.

It was just getting dark when we arrived, and as we walked down a cracked asphalt path and shined our plastic flashlights on the overgrown grass and rampant bushes everywhere, I was surprised at how much worse it looked than in my memory. Whatever half-hearted efforts had been made in the past to maintain the park seemed to have been given up now, as though a decision had been reached to just let the space return to nature through the slow process of urban decay.

We were getting close to the splintery skeleton of the bridge when Steve poked me in the ribs. "Look over there!" he whispered, his hand now tight on my arm. "I think that's the man!" I turned my light toward where he was looking and illuminated an old, rusted out water fountain that was next to the path further head.

Jack snickered. "Good looking out, Stevie. Let us know if you see any rabid squirrels or trashcan monsters too."

I laughed a little, but it was forced. I didn't really think there was some dangerous man out here, much less a ghost, but I had to admit the park was creepy. Unsettling even. I wasn't willing to be made fun of by asking to leave before we were done looking around, but I did pick up my pace. If we made it all the way through, I reasoned, we could all go home without the danger of being called a chicken.

Looking back on it, I think some dim part of me realized we were being followed early on. Some primitive instinct that recognized that something wasn't right. But it wasn't until we were passing under the bridge that I heard the rustle of someone walking a few feet behind us. I still don't know why I didn't just bolt right then, but for whatever reason I stopped and turned. My friends lurched to a halt and spun around as well, with Jack letting out a gasp as he saw what was behind us.

It…It looked like a man, but it wasn't a man. The outline was that of a large person wearing a big poncho or hooded overcoat, so if you just caught a glimpse, you would think it was just a tall, broad-chested man out for a walk. But when I shined my light on it…

It was made of rot. I saw mounds of dirt run through with worms and maggots, bits of trash stuck to the decaying carcasses of mice and birds, strings of brown ichor wound tight round hot, red meat that never stopped moving and pulsing as it slid around on what approximated the thing's chest and face. Its eyes were irregular circles of broken green glass, and the bits of bottle seemed to shine with some dull inner light as it regarded us. But none of that was the worst of it.

When it opened its mouth to speak, I saw it had long, thin teeth of silver. It took me a moment to realize what they were. Hypodermic needles.

"Do you have somethin' ta offer?" Its voice was deep and roaring, like the wind of an angry storm. We all took a step back that it matched with a shambling step forward. "Or do you mean ta waste m'time?"

We ran. Of course we ran. I could hear it behind us, somehow moving, somehow gaining on us as we tried to make it out of the park. Its footfalls were heavy and squelching, and when I realized they were getting closer, I looked back just as it reached Steve. I saw it when it closed a wriggling, oozing hand on Steve's shoulder, and I heard the start of Steve's terrified wail as he registered the contact. But then the scream was cut off. Because Steve wasn't there anymore.

Let me be very clear on this point. It wasn't as though I lost sight of him or he turned and went a different way. I watched him literally disappear in front of my eyes — clothes and candy bag and everything that was him. I even heard a faint popping sound as air rushed in to fill the void his absence created.

The sight of it almost made me stop dead in my tracks. It made no sense. What had happened to him? It was as if my brain wanted to reconcile what it had just seen before it could go back to the pressing business of running away from the horror that was chasing us. But I caught myself, and I didn't stop. I just slowed down for a couple of seconds. That was just enough time for Jack to plow into me and knock us both down.

I had the breath knocked out of me, but my fear and panic had reasserted itself and I was immediately pushing myself up to run again. That's when I heard another small popping sound right behind me. I looked back to see that Jack was gone now too. The monster was standing over me, its green eyes blazing as it scraped its metal teeth back and forth.

"Do you have somethin' ta offer?" Its voice filled my ears and I felt my pants grow warm as I wet myself.

I shook my head as I began to cry. "N-no. All I have is this." I held out the empty trick-or-treat bag in my right hand. I had lost my flashlight when Jack ran into me, so I really had nothing else to offer the thing. Or so I thought.

It suddenly shot out its hands and gripped my right arm, and after a moment of tingling pain, it was gone. My arm, all the way up to the shoulder, was just gone. I watched in amazed horror as the empty bag fluttered to the ground now that it had no hand to support it. Reaching up, I touched my shoulder, finding only smooth skin where the start of my arm should be. It was as though it had never been there at all. When I looked back up, I saw the creature giving me a terrible, shining smile.

"Fairly paid. You may go." With that, it turned and walked back into the shadows where it disappeared.

I ran all the way back home, and I didn't stop running

until I was crying in my mother's arms while my father called the police. They believed me that I had been attacked, but they didn't understand the rest. The stuff about the monster was clearly because I was in shock, but how did they explain these other people I was making up? Or how I now claimed I had always had a right arm before that night?

Because Jack Paulson and Steve Marks weren't just missing. They didn't exist at all anymore. Just like my arm, no one had any memory or evidence of my two best friends ever existing, not even their own families. Even my own memory of Jack had gaps, and I think it's because I actually saw Steve disappear, but only heard when the thing got Jack.

But I was the only one that remembered them at all. For weeks I kept waiting for something to change, for someone to tell the truth or suddenly remember them again. But it never happened. Instead, I spent the next several years getting increasingly intensive therapy as my parents drew away from me more and more. Eventually, I learned to lie and keep the truth of what happened to myself…well, except for Abigail, but we know how that turned out.

I'm ashamed to say that I lied to myself for a number of years too. Tried to just believe that I had some mental issues and a birth defect. That the best way of getting past it was to accept that I was wrong and the world was right. Problem was, I never really believed it. In my heart, I've always known what happened to my friends.

What I don't know is why or how. I don't know what that thing is, and I don't want to know. I never went back, never tried to investigate…nothing like that. In part, because I didn't think I'd get anywhere. In part, because even today I'm fucking terrified of that thing.

Anyway, that's the real story of how I lost my arm. Thank you for listening and not laughing or calling a doctor.

You're a good kid.

****

Four weeks later, Peter was dead. He wanted to be cremated, with his ashes to go to his mother, an elderly woman who was still alive and living in Westerfield. He had no other family or friends, and his mother was too feeble to come get the remains, so I volunteered to carry them down the next day for a small service she was going to have in his honor.

The trip down was uneventful, and the service was nice, if very sparsely attended. At the end, I gave his mother a brief hug and told her again how much Peter had meant to me, surprising myself by realizing it was the truth. He had been a good friend, and while I didn't believe his crazy story about Amerson Park, I did think the world was a worse place without him in it.

It was late afternoon as I turned out onto the highway that would take me home. Peter was right. I had never been to Westerfield before, and as I traveled through it, I found myself imagining Peter growing up there. The thing was, I kept imagining him with Jack and Steve. I knew it was just a mental trick—I knew next to nothing about his childhood, and what I did know came from him and included these fictional friends. It was only natural that I would insert them into my own…

Amerson Park

The sign was small and rusted, with such a pronounced lean that the name and arrow were barely legible from the road. But I felt my heart leap when it caught my eye, and before I knew it I was backing up a few feet to make the turn down into a decrepit part of old Westerfield. As I drove slowly down the patchy stretch of street, I told myself that visiting the park was a good way of honoring the part of Peter that he had to keep hidden from the world.

And that was true. But I also wanted to see the park for

myself. Prove to myself that it was just a story. So I parked outside a chain-link fence that was rusted to the point of collapse and made my way into the park. It was getting dark, but I could still see well-enough to make out the main features. It was surprisingly close to the way I had imagined it when Peter was telling me his story. I saw the path they had walked, the remnants of the water fountain Steve had been scared of, and in the distance, the silhouette of what had once been a small wooden walking bridge.

I threaded my way gingerly through the tall grass, my fear of getting snake-bit walking hand-in-hand with my nervousness at being in this place. My goal was to make it to the bridge, look under it, maybe take a picture or two, and then leave before full night came on. The air was already turning cooler, and the October light was fading faster than I'd expected. And I was getting close to the bridge, but it was already getting harder to make it out in the growing pool of shadows.

That's when one of the shadows stepped away from the rest.

It was just like Peter had described. A tall, large man shape wearing a long coat or cloak of some kind with a hood. I slowed to a stop, my brain frantically trying to come up with a reasonable explanation for what I was seeing. But then I saw them. Its glowing, green glass eyes, burning in the moving darkness of its head like twin lanterns. And below that, I thought I saw the pale glint of silver in the failing autumn sun.

I ran. I ran and didn't look back, jumping the fence and driving away before that terrible thing could reach me, touch me, take me away. I drove without stopping until I got home, almost wrecking more than once in my frantic desire to just get far away from that place and what lived there. That was a few days ago, and I think I may be safe. I also think I might be going insane.

You see, I keep having memories that can't be right. I remember having a girlfriend. I think her name was Angelica, and I have several snippets of spending time with her. Loving her even. There are times when I can picture her face or imagine what her voice was like. There are times when I can almost remember things I did with her. Our first date, bowling, meeting her parents.

Her going with me to Peter's funeral.

It's probably all in my head. I'm a big believer that people can trick themselves into believing just about anything. Missing arms, monsters under the bridge, girlfriends that no longer exist. I probably just need to take some time off and get my head right.

Maybe then I'll stop imagining I heard her scream as I scrambled over the fence at Amerson Park, never looking back to see what happened to her. Maybe then I won't remember feeling that brief change in the air as a void at my back was created and then filled. Maybe then I can stop looking out of my windows every night, half-expecting to see green glass shining at me from somewhere in the dark, waiting patiently to finish some terrible transaction.

Maybe.

The Shadow Game

"Happy Halloween…almost. Are you ready to party down?"

Chuck patted me on the shoulder as he asked the question, moving past me through the front door without getting a response. The question seemed well-meant, as was most everything that Chuck did or said around me. It said that he cared enough to come to this party he probably didn't want to be at and to ask a jovial question as he came in, but I knew that was about the threshold of his caring. We weren't friends, not really, and it was our mutual love of my sister Vanessa that had led to our lives intersecting at all.

She was next through the door, giving me a tight hug while trying not to drop the bowl of dip she was balancing in her right hand. She whispered in my ear, "You doing okay? This okay?" and I squeezed her back as I replied, "Yeah, Ness. I'm good. This is good."

When Billy showed up twenty minutes later, it was less awkward. He had been my best friend for nearly twenty years, and I had talked more to him about everything than I had anyone else in the time since Amber had died. When I opened the door, he just gave me a quick man hug and started talking to Vanessa and Chuck as I went to finish arranging the chairs in the living room.

****

My wife Amber died six months ago. She had always been a fairly healthy person, but a year earlier she had started feeling bad. She was diagnosed with Type II diabetes, which at the time, seemed like bad but very manageable news. Then one weekend I was away for a work trip. Amber had talked about coming with me, but I'd been afraid she'd be bored and encouraged her to stay home and relax instead. She agreed and said she would see about having Vanessa and Chuck over for dinner that Saturday night.

Her and Vanessa had become best friends in the six years we had been married, and she typically talked to my sister more than I did. But between occasional visits and texts, I almost never talked to my sister on the phone. So when I woke up at one in the morning to my phone buzzing and saw it was Vanessa, I knew something was wrong.

The coroner ruled it a "sudden cardiac death" with diabetes listed as a contributing factor. It was a rare thing for someone in their mid-thirties, but apparently it did happen from time to time. Vanessa told me that they had all three fallen asleep watching a movie, and when she woke up, she and Chuck tried to get Amber up to tell her they were heading home. But she wouldn't wake up. They called 911 and she was declared dead at the scene.

Since then, everything had been a red blur of anger and sadness. I didn't want to be around anyone. I found it hard to work or interact with people, and every day I rushed home to solitude as soon as I was able, because it was suffocating being around others. I always felt like a fish struggling to get back to water, desperately striving to get back to our home and away from everything else.

In the back of my mind, I expected things to get better over time. For the order and monotony of day-to-day life to abrade away the rough edges of my grief and leave me with a heavy stone that would never leave, but was at least easier to carry. But that didn't happen. My memories of her didn't fade. I kept forgetting she was gone. I would hear something in another part of the house and have a moment where I assumed it was her before I remembered. I would walk into a room and swear that I could still smell her there.

Don't misunderstand me. I don't think she was haunting me or anything. I just think that my mind couldn't cope with the reality that she was dead — and in some corner of my heart, I was slowly deciding I didn't want any part of this reality anymore.

That's when I got the phone call from the real estate agent. Amber's aunt had died two years earlier, and having no children of her own, she had left Amber everything. That consisted mainly of her house, a little money in the bank, and a pawn shop she had run for almost forty years. Nearly all of the estate had been dealt with before Amber passed away — Aunt's house was bought by a young married couple and the items in the pawn shop were all auctioned off or sold in lots to other shops. Only the pawn shop itself was left to be sold, and because it had been important to Amber to see it all done, it was one of the few things I had dedicated myself to since she died.

I managed to find a buyer, and the property closing had happened just a couple of days before the real estate agent called me. He said that the new owners had found an item hidden behind a false wall in a storage closet at the shop. The agent told me they could have claimed it themselves since the purchase was done, and the object in question was clearly old and potentially very valuable, but that the pair that bought the shop were honest and didn't feel right about keeping something I most likely hadn't known existed when I sold them the shop.

I forced myself to listen to what the agent was telling me, but when he was done, I told him to keep it himself then. I didn't care. I had a rapidly dwindling to-do list, and once that was done, I wasn't sure how long I would be around anyway.

But he told me it was already on its way. Sure enough, it was delivered the following day. And while I opened the large and heavy box out of habit more than interest, that changed when I saw what was inside.

I held up the large card that had come taped to the top of the object when I opened it. It was filled with small, cramped cursive that was nonetheless legible as I held it up to a nearby lamp in the living room. Chuck and Vanessa were already sitting down in the chairs I had arranged around the box itself, while Billy stood some distance off sipping a beer. All of them looked interested but slightly concerned by the set-up and the strange-looking box, but I gave a reassuring smile and told them this was going to be our "Halloween game" for the evening. Ignoring their concerned glances at me and the box, I began to read the card aloud.

"This item is the Izu Box of Shadows. My research has shown there are other boxes, although they appear to be very rare and all from different places and times. This box was made in the Izu Province of what is now the Shizuoka Prefecture in Japan. While I cannot be certain, this item appears to have been made between 1750 and 1800. I have been unable to ascertain the nature of all components of the box, but its basic composition is of heavily lacquered wood and metal. The inner mechanical workings of the box have never been maintained — or even viewed — since I came into possession of the box, but in my experience they always work smoothly and without fail."

I stepped closer to the box. I had it sitting on a low table in the center of a ring of four chairs. The box was a two-foot tall hexagon of black wood with grayish-brown metal securing every edge. It was largely unadorned, with no writing or symbols on its surface — though occasionally I thought you could see the ghost of some marking deep within its dark skin. But while its surfaces appeared plain, the top of the box was not.

The highest portion of each of the six sides was occupied by a long, rounded glass rectangle trimmed in the same storm cloud metal. These were its viewing slots. The top of the box slanted on every side up to a peak at its center that held a perforated metal cap. The cap reminded me of the top of a giant salt shaker, though with fewer holes and with grooves at the edge of the cap to provide a better grip. This cap was screwed on top of a metal tube that ran down into the center of the box and out of sight. Touching this center metal axle, I continued to read.

"The box is used as follows: One to six people may participate, but everyone who is in the room must participate and it can be no more than six. To begin, the center metal tube is uncapped. If you look inside the tube you will see a red candle. Important: Only use this candle and do not worry about its depletion."

I glanced up and saw all three of them were looking at me and the box with more interest now, though the worry was still there as well. Turning back to the card, I went on.

"Pull up on the edge of the tube and you will find that this portion lifts out easily. This is the candle portion. Remember to reseat that portion properly when you put the tube back in a moment, as the tube must be placed back within its grooves in order for the box to function properly. After you remove the candle portion of the tube, you will find a small compartment below. This is where the personal objects are housed during the box's use."

"The objects must be very small, of course, but almost any item the person possesses will work. Buttons and coins are common, though hair or teeth can be used as well. The only real criteria are possession by the user, only one item per person, and something small enough that all the objects can be fit inside at the same time. The amount of objects will, of course, vary by the number of participants."

"After the items are placed in the bottom chamber of the tube, the candle portion is replaced and the candle is lit. The cap is then screwed on tightly. You are now ready to begin."

I sat down in one of the empty chairs and gestured for Billy to do the same. He frowned and took a step forward, but hesitated. "What is this, man? Some kind of séance or something? I'll help however you need, but I just don't know how healthy…"

"It's not a fucking séance, okay? Just…" I paused and took a breath. I needed to keep my cool. "I just need you all to keep an open mind. I'm not trying to contact Amber or something. But it's a weird thing and I thought it'd be cool to share it with my friends. I was nervous to try it out alone."

Vanessa reached over and squeezed my arm. For his part, Billy blushed a little before flopping down in the chair next to me. "Shit, man. I'm sorry. I'll do whatever you need." Nodding to him, I looked back to the card.

"The first participant puts his eyes to his viewing slot and then grasps the metal tube cap. He then spins the central tube counterclockwise and lets go. If done properly, the participant will see something remarkable, though what that is varies greatly from person to person. Only one spin is required, and when their view darkens again, their turn is complete. This continues until everyone has completed a turn. A second turn can be done, but is very ill-advised. Under no circumstances are you to tell another participant what you saw while viewings are still being conducted."

I looked up and smiled. "That's it. Now. Are you ready to party down?"

****

All the personal items were put in the box and then Billy went. He seemed to be debating what object to use at first, but then he pulled a small pumpkin eraser out of his pocket. Smiling with embarrassment, he shrugged. "A patient gave it to me. Being a pediatrician has its perks."

When he spun the central tube, I saw both Vanessa and Chuck jerk back slightly at the sound it made. It was an odd, lonely rasping sound not unlike what you hear on a night filled with cicadas. My sister glanced at me with a frown and mouthed "what is this thing?" as Billy continued to lean forward against the viewing slot, the hollow whirr of the tube beginning to slow down. I just smiled and gave a shrug before turning back to watch Billy.

After more than a minute, Billy sat back and blinked as though he were coming out of a cave. His eyes were unfocused as he looked at me. "What the fuck was that, man? How is that even possible?"

Chuck glanced around the box at Billy. "What did you see?" Vanessa poked him in the side.

"No telling what you saw, remember?" She looked over at Billy. "You okay, though?"

Billy rubbed his eyes and nodded. "Yeah...Yeah I just...Don't mind me. Go ahead and go."

Chuck went next, having put in a dime from his pocket. He had just spun the tube when Billy stood up and stumbled back. "I...I think I got motion sick or something. I don't feel well. I should go."

I looked away from Chuck and shook my head. "It'll pass probably. Plus, if you're woozy, the last thing you need to be doing is driving a car. Why don't you just go lay down for a few minutes while we do the rest of the turns? You're already done."

Billy looked at me for several seconds as though he was weighing something, and I was on the verge of saying more when he nodded. "Yeah, okay. I'll try that for a minute. But no promises."

I looked back to see that Chuck's spinning of the tube

was coming to an end, but when it was done he didn't lean back or say anything. Vanessa looked at me questioningly. "Something is wrong."

I frowned. "Yeah, I don't know. Hey, Chuck?" When he still didn't respond, Vanessa shook his shoulder and then gave him a light shove. This seemed to rouse him enough that he sat back and looked at us sheepishly.

"Um, sorry guys. I think I fell asleep against that thing. It's been a long week at work."

Vanessa stared at him. "You're telling me you fell full asleep in the three minutes you were messing with it? With your face leaned up against this weird box?"

He shrugged. "I guess. I just…Look, I hate to be the party pooper, but can we go ahead and go, honey?" Chuck glanced at me. "I'm sorry, man. I want to hang out tonight, but I'm kind of with Billy. I don't feel so great now."

I stood up. "I'm sorry, man. Want me to see if I have anything for your head or motion sickness or something?"

He shook his head as he started to rise to his feet. "No, I think I just need to go home actually. We can do this some other night."

I looked down at my sister. "Ness, please don't go. I'm sorry this isn't going well, but I'm really trying here. It took a lot for me to even invite you guys over at all."

She bit her lip and glanced at Chuck, then back to me. "I know. I know." She looked at the box and then turned to her husband. "Look, let's stay a bit longer. Go lay down and I'll finish playing the game. If you don't start feeling better in a bit, we'll go, I promise." Chuck went to argue, but Vanessa was already leaning forward and spinning.

Chuck gave me a hard look before moving to the sofa I had pushed back against a far wall of the living room. I could feel his eyes burning a hole through my back, but I tried to ignore it. I didn't want to miss Vanessa's reaction. I didn't have long to wait, as after just a few seconds she began to speak in a high, loud voice on the edge of a scream.

"Hell is a forest deep and dark. Its earth is cold, its trees are stark. Among the shades dwells the Hunter's face, please send another in my place."

She said the words in a rush and then trailed off like a burned-out engine winding down as she slid out of her chair and onto the floor. Chuck was already on his feet, and when he saw her begin to thrash silently on the ground, he moved past me to help her. It was easy to stick the stun gun into his side and send him crashing down to flop next to his wife like a dying fish.

I couldn't be sure what was happening to Vanessa or how long it would last, but I knew I only had a few seconds before Chuck would be back up. Before the guests arrived, I had taped a long-bladed butcher knife under the table holding the box—one of several weapons I had squirrelled away for different possible scenarios that evening. Now I yanked it free from its hiding spot as I moved on top of my brother-in-law. He was already regaining control and tried to grab my arm, but he was too slow. I slammed the knife into his Adam's apple and gave it a strong twist.

"That's for Amber, you motherfucker."

He flailed around for a handful of heartbeats, but when I pulled the knife free and sent it back across his throat with all my weight, his hands fell to the ground like dead birds. One look at his eyes and I knew he was gone. Good.

Looking over at Vanessa, I saw she had stopped convulsing, but she wasn't moving other than breathing heavily. At least she wasn't dead yet. I remember having the thought at that moment that everything was going so well because what I was doing was right. Righteous even. Amber wasn't perfect, but she didn't deserve what they did to her, and they were all going to pay.

Standing up from Chuck, I wiped the knife off on my pants leg and moved to the bedroom where Billy should be. I had to assume he might be aware of what had happened in the living room, so I was tensed and ready for an attack as I pushed open the bedroom door. Flipping on the light with the hand holding the stun gun, I looked for some sign of him, but there was none.

Cursing under my breath, I almost went back out into the hall before noticing the bathroom door was closed and the light was on. I listened at the door for a minute, but everything was quiet. Looking behind me for any potential ambush, I called out to Billy as though I was checking on him, seeing if he was sick in the bathroom. Nothing.

I twisted the knob and it didn't budge. Locked. That was okay. The door was flimsy and nothing was going to keep me from finishing what I had started. Two kicks and the door flew open. I stepped forward and peered into the room, initially confused at what I was seeing. Billy was laying in the empty bathtub, dead. He had used the pocket knife he always carried to slit his wrists both horizontally and vertically, and judging from how much blood was pooled under him, he had either done it almost immediately after leaving us or had just bled out very quickly. Either way, I said a silent word of thanks to the box. Billy was larger and stronger than me, so I had expected the most trouble from him. Apparently whatever he had seen in the box of shadows had been enough to convince him he needed to do the right thing after all.

Going back into the living room, I saw that Vanessa was starting to come around. She was up on all fours, trying to pull herself up into a chair but failing miserably. It didn't help when I took my foot and shoved her in the side, sending her rolling back down onto her back. When she looked up at me, I saw that she had small dots of blood at the corners of her eyes.

"So what did you see?"

She just looked at me confusedly as though she either didn't recognize me or didn't understand the words I was saying. I crouched down and gave her face a hard slap.

"Snap out of it. I want you to understand what's gone on before you die."

She sucked in a breath at the slap, and when she looked back at me, I saw recognition. She looked past me to where Chuck lay dead and the first real emotion came back to her face. Her eyes went back to mine as pink tears began to run down her cheeks.

"Why? What have you done?"

I slapped her again. "What have I done? What have you done. What have all of you done." I felt an almost overpowering urge to go ahead and stab her, so I stood up and walked a few feet away. "I saw what you did. The box showed me what you did."

Vanessa still looked dazed, and her words slurred slightly as she spoke, but she furrowed her brow and managed to get out: "What? We didn't do anything."

I let out a bitter laugh. "Well, I guess that's kind of true, isn't it?" I gripped the knife so hard I could feel the bones in my hand groan in protest. "The box showed me the night Amber died. How you, and Chuck, and Billy came over. How you drugged Amber. Got her drunk. Did obscene, perverted things with her, all of you. And then when she collapsed from everything you had given her…when she started dying, you all just stood around and laughed. Didn't get her help. Didn't try to save her. You just watched her die while you all fucking laughed."

I was closer again, standing over Vanessa and screaming the last of it, my own tears streaming now. She was talking again, trying to say it wasn't true. That it was insane and made no sense. But I knew she was lying. I knew what the box had shown me. I knew the truth.

So I killed my baby sister. I wish I could say I didn't remember it, but it would be a lie. I know every blow that fell, every scream she made, every moment of joy and fulfillment I felt at causing her pain and avenging what had happened to my sweet Amber. It was all so clear and perfect.

But when it was over, that clarity began to fade. I sat in the floor of my living room, covered in blood and feeling doubt and fear sliding into my belly like the blade I had left in the ruined remains of Vanessa. Why was I so sure I could trust what the box had shown me? Wouldn't the autopsy of Amber have shown drugs and alcohol in her system if it had happened like I saw? And why would any of them want to do any of that in the first place?

Within a few minutes I went from exultation to despair. I still felt confused, and even now I can't say for sure what makes sense and what doesn't, but I think I've been tricked. As I've been writing all this out, my head has cleared further. I think maybe I've murdered the only people I had left, the only ones that cared about me at all.

Even the beginnings of that realization filled me with a burning desire to kill myself. I likely would have done it then, but something unexpected stopped me. My phone rang, and when I answered, it was you.

"Hello? Is this Mr. Saltzmann?"

I nodded dumbly and then realized I needed to speak. "Yes. I guess."

"Hi there. My name is Cora Westgate. I've been trying to track you down. Or at least something I think you have." You paused for me to reply, but I sat silent, so you went on. "It's a box. It's called an…Izu Box of Shadows, I think?"

I almost hung up then. This was delaying me pulling the knife from my sister's corpse and using it on myself. But something made me ask the question anyway.

"Why do you want it?"

I heard excitement in your voice. "So you do have it. Awesome. Look, my uncle…he's been abducted. By very bad people. And I think the box can help me find him. I know that sounds crazy, but if…"

"Fine." I was surprised to hear the word come out of my mouth and I could tell you were surprised too.

"Oh, wow. Great! Look, I have your address and I can be there in two hours if that's okay. I'll be glad to pay you well for it but…"

"No, I won't be here when you get here. Just take it." Again, I didn't know why I was still talking to you, much less why I was encouraging you to take something that I was feeling more and more sure was the cause of all the horror around me.

You were trying to thank me, but I was already hanging up. I almost went for the knife then, but some part of me, the real me, hesitated. I knew I wanted to die, but I wanted to warn you as best I could. If I couldn't say it to you, maybe writing out what happened would work. I expected to not be able to even start telling it, much less finish it. I thought the box wouldn't let me tell you. Warn you.

But now that I'm done, I think I understand. The box wants to go with you, and while it knows you will read this, it also knows you won't heed my warning. I can only hope that it's wrong.

Please do not take the box. Or if you do, don't use it. Destroy it if you can. You'll find me dead, find us all dead, and maybe you'll believe that I didn't mean to do any of it. If you know about things like the box, you may be the only one that might understand. Either way, it's done now. Tricked or not, I think I might be damned.

Cora, please don't use the box. Please believe that I'm sorry for what I did.

I love you, Amber. I hope to make it back to you some day.

Goodbye.

Uncle Teddy and Cora: The Cost of Doing Business

The worst car accident I've ever been in before last month was when I was thirteen. My father was taking us to a local steakhouse for dinner when someone rear-ended our car. It was jarring, and we all yelled, but only out of surprise and momentary fear, not because we were hurt. Within thirty minutes we were back on our way to the restaurant, those few seconds of uncertainty and worry left behind us on the road.

When the truck hit us last week, it was entirely different. Our SUV took the hit well all things considered, but the truck weighed twice as much as we did and was t-boning us at a high speed. I was driving, with Teddy in the passenger seat per usual. Heckle and Jeckle, just recently repaired from their bloody work at the Rajah theater, were sitting silent in the back seat, also per usual.

What was not usual was suddenly having the road flip away from us like a page in a children's pop-up story book. I actually noticed that before my body registered the impact and the world-filling noise of the truck slamming into us hard enough to send us rolling off the road and down the embankment to our right. I saw the world spin once, twice, and Teddy was yelling something to the magpie twins, but it was too late. My world was already being replaced by darkness.

I couldn't have been out more than a few seconds, but when I came to Heckle was pulling me free from the car. My vision was blurry, but I managed to focus in on the sound of Teddy's voice, his ill-defined shape standing some distance away between me and the group assembled up at the top of the hill.

"...go with you, but you leave her alone. Unless you want to see how difficult I can really be."

The people he was talking to were little more than dark silhouettes to my bleary eyes—a fact not helped by the deepening blue of twilight. But the laugh of one of them was more easy to define. Distinctly feminine, disdainful, and cruel.

"You're not in a position to make threats, Mr. Westgate. Surely you understand who we represent?"

I saw Uncle Teddy take a couple of steps forward. "Half of you look like undertaker bodybuilders. The other half look like someone put an all-you-can-eat buffet at a death metal concert. So I'm guessing you're all douchebags working for the Blind Court. Putting your peanut butter and jelly of physical and magical violence together to try and make a threatening sandwich."

The woman's voice was colder this time. "Cute. We'll see how cute you are when..." Her words were cut off as Jeckle thundered past Teddy and was up the hill in a second. I saw the person I thought was the woman who'd been talking dive out of the way, but she wasn't fast enough.

Jeckle grabbed her left arm and yanked her back close enough that he could get a grip on her left leg as well. Then, with what seemed like very little effort at all, he began to shake her against the ground like an old blanket while she screamed. The noise she made was strange, seeming to come in waves as she went up and down, stopping briefly as she struck the ground before renewing in a more pathetic, wetter form. By the fourth time against the ground, she was silent. By the sixth, her arm and leg had come off in Jeckle's massive hands. I could make out him looking at the freed appendages with what I imagined was bemusement before casually dropping them and walking back down to stand by Teddy's side.

"Now who wants to be the new spokesperson?" Teddy's

voice was light, but underneath ran a thread of danger that made me suppress a shudder. Still, what was he talking about? Letting them take him? Fuck that.

I went to stand up but realized for the first time that my left arm, which had been numb, was starting to throb painfully now. Looking down at it, I blinked when I realized it was at an odd angle. Fuck. I don't have time for this. Resigning myself to sitting up, I yelled hoarsely to Teddy.

"You're not going with them. What're you talking about?"

My vision was clearing somewhat, and I could see Teddy's face when he turned around. He was angry and sad, but he was scared too. He wasn't going to show that to them, but he let it slip for a second when he looked at me. "Cora, don't argue with me." He gestured back at the people up the hill, most of whom were standing in mute shock as they listened to us bicker or picked pieces of their cohort off themselves. "Yes, we could kill them. They're clearly incompetent. But what about the next group? Or the next group after that? The Blind Court isn't incompetent, and they'll eventually send someone that beats us. At least this way I know you're safe."

I could feel my eyes starting to fill with tears. He was serious. "No. That's bullshit. We can beat them. We can beat all of them."

Teddy gave me a sad smile and shook his head. "No. You can't beat everybody. The key is knowing when to fight and when not to." He looked back up the hill. "Do we have a deal, or will I have to make this offer to whoever they send next?"

A short, heavily-muscled man with a silvery crewcut stepped forward and nodded. "Deal. Come with us and the rest can go."

Teddy nodded. "Just a moment and I'll be ready."

Turning back to me, I saw his own eyes were shining in the lights from the car. "I'm so proud of you, Cora. So happy we had this time together. But you need to remember what I would want you to do. I would never risk you to save myself. I don't want you wasting time boxing at shadows. And it may be tempting to look up some of my old contacts for leads, but it would be a waste of good currency that is better used elsewhere. Honest Abe, I'm telling you the truth. Spend that beast where it's actually of use. Ok?"

I stared at him. "What the fuck are you talking about? And by the way, you risk me to save yourself on the reg."

He rolled his eyes and spoke in an irritated whisper. "I was trying to be cleverly cryptic. I see now that my nuanced coded message was lost on you. Look in the devil pig, okay? And fast is better." I was going to ask another question, but he raised his hand to stop me. "Everything I said was true. Love you." Wiping at his eyes, he turned and walked up toward his captors.

I looked at Heckle and Jeckle. "Go get him back. Kill the rest of them." They started lurching forward immediately, but Teddy turned and shook his head. The golems immediately stopped again.

"No. You stay with her and protect her. Don't listen to her until I'm gone with them. After that, you only listen to her." He looked over at the nearby group of what I could now tell looked like a mixed bag of mercenaries and occultists—all of who were giving him a wide berth now. "And if anyone tries to mess with her, ever, you fucking tear them apart." He gave me a little wave before glancing down at Crew-cut. "Lead the way."

I yelled after him, but it did no good. Jeckle picked me up gently, and after waiting a few moments for them to leave with Teddy, they began walking with me toward what Heckle told me in his clipped fashion was the nearest hospital. I wondered how they knew where they were going and contemplated if magpies had good senses of direction. They walked at a steady but fast pace along the road as it began to drizzle and then pour. I didn't care. I felt exhausted. Used up. So I lay my head against Jeckle's chest and let my tears mix in with the falling rain as we traveled through the dark.

****

Two hours later and I was back at Teddy's house. The hospital had wanted me to stay longer, but I had no time to waste. My arm wasn't going to be less broken because I sat through more of their bullshit, and I had to find out what Teddy was trying to tell me.

I knew what he meant by "devil pig". He had a massive ceramic boar with large stag horns growing out of its head in his bedroom. It was so hideous that it kind of circled back around to being cute. When I got back home and went to get it, I realized it had two other traits I hadn't noticed before. First, it was very heavy — I was barely able to carry it with my one good arm. Second, it had a large slit opening in the middle of its back.

It was a piggy bank.

I looked for another opening, but there was none. Hoping I was doing the right thing, I scooped the devil pig off the table it was sitting on and lugged it over to the stone fireplace. It broke cleanly into two pieces when I dropped it, and I felt confusion and worry when I saw what had been inside.

It was tumerin. The evil-looking boar had been filled to the brim with hundreds of the dark, oblong-shaped coins that had once served as the currency of infernal Hell. But how were they useful now? And how did it help me know what to do next?

I sucked in a breath as I saw a slip of paper sticking out

of one of the scattered piles of coins. Pulling it free, I saw it was a note written in Teddy's handwriting. It said:

People I trust (in the order that I trust them):

1. Cora (imagine a smiley-faced emoji)

2. Abraham McMillen (a dark practitioner, but not like the ones we're after. Plus, he owes me. But, still watch him.)

3. Olivia Height (a good person. If things go wrong, find her and she can help hide you. Otherwise, she should be kept out of this. She doesn't have the stomach for it.)

Below you will find their contact information. If the Blind Court has me, I don't know how time works there, so be quick. I do have a plan, but it's somewhat improvisational, as all my best plans are. And I still need your help, so do your best.

For inspiration, I have included a quote from that song you continue to play despite my very subtle hints that it is abhorrent.

"Because baby you're a firework. Come on show them what you're worth."

May Ms. Perry's words inspire you to get me the fuck out of here.

Love,

Teddy

****

I hit the buzzer for the third time. I was outside of an older townhouse apartment in Boston, but it was in good condition and I had no illusions that the buzzer or intercom didn't work. Either "Honest Abe" wasn't there or he was ignoring me, and I had a feeling I knew which. Pressing down the intercom button again, I leaned close to keep my voice low.

"Listen, Mr. McMillen. You can hang up when I call, you can try to ignore me now, but I'm going to get your help. Teddy said you were one of his only real friends."

There was a crackle and then a deep voice with a faint Scottish accent came over the intercom. "That's a lie. He doesn't have friends. He has people he still thinks are useful and those he's already used up. You'd do well to steer clear of him and whatever deviltry he's gotten into this time."

I thumbed the button again. "That may be, but he's my uncle. And maybe he's not your friend, but he does think he can trust you to help. And since you're kind of only my only option, I'm asking for you to please let me up."

Crackle. "You're not listening, girl. I'm not interested in you or him. Sorry you wasted your time."

Gritting my teeth, I stabbed my finger at the button. "Listen, motherfucker. I hope you like your shitty apartment, because you're going to be in there a long time. And when you finally get sick of it and come out, I'll still be here waiting. And if you still decide you don't want to help me, you'll fucking find out what happens when I don't have a use for you any more."

There was a pause and then: "Jesus. Okay. You really are his niece, fuck. Come on up."

The door buzzed and I went through it, Heckle following dutifully behind me. I don't blame the golems for what happened next. Heckle was focused on me and any threats ahead, and Jeckle was back at the car around the corner. Neither of them noticed the smoky form that followed us inside the townhouse anymore than I did. None of us realized the death that had been stalking me for some time.

Until it was too late.

Uncle Teddy and Cora: Breakfast with the Blind Court

"Ted? Wake up, honey. Breakfast is ready."

I'd already started waking up before she spoke, but I made a point of getting up slowly at the sound of the lilting, female voice. Stretching, I rubbed my face before opening my eyes to see a version of Rebecca in front of me. I had last seen her more than thirty years ago, and this version could have aged that much, though she looked closer to forty years than my fifty-five. We had already broken up before I left town to pursue my idiotic dreams of becoming the hottest new artist on the west coast, and I never contacted her again, even after I became the most successful dollmaker in the world.

Some of that was because my success as a dollmaker made me very dangerous to be around. The people I worked for wanted to keep me separate from any personal connections or potential Jimmy the Cricket consciences on my shoulder, and I had learned that people I got close to had a tendency of disappearing. But most of it was because I knew that Rebecca had died of ovarian cancer when we were 37.

"Hi there, Becks. You're looking well. Very well indeed." I tipped a wink at whatever this thing in front of me actually was, trying to keep the hurt and anger out of my voice. "So what's the deal here, huh?"

Rebecca was wearing a nightgown that was sheer enough to show the outlines of her body as she sat down on the edge of the bed and leaned towards me with the bright, mischievous smile I had always loved so much. "Well, I fixed us a big breakfast, but beyond that, the deal is whatever you want it to be, Teddy."

I noticed that she had no smell. That was interesting, because that meant that wherever they got their information to make this version of Rebecca, it hadn't come from my memories. Smell is always a strong part of memory, and that was especially true for my memories of Rebecca. We had both grown up on the poor side of middle class, and while neither of us could afford fancy clothes or cars, I remember she always smelled like the perfect combination of soap, this lavender-scented perfume she liked, and another sweet smell that was just her. But when they constructed this thing, they decided to err on the side of caution and not get the wrong smell because they couldn't access my memories of what would be right.

That meant the tumerin were doing their job. Good.

I sat up in bed and eased past her to stand up. "Well, let's see what we've got for breakfast then."

I found myself being led through a generically beautiful house that was well-furnished and had windows looking out onto a rolling green lawn that appeared to be bordered by a road of dark earth leading off to somewhere out of sight. There was no way of knowing if any of that was actually real or just essentially a fancy magical screensaver, but time would tell.

We had reached a breakfast nook at the edge of what appeared to be a large kitchen, and the table was filled with a variety of eggs, bacon, waffles and tater-tots. It was the tots that got me. Giving the abomination that looked like Rebecca a smile, I sat down and started digging in.

After I was through my second plate, I sat back with a contented sigh. "That was a very tasty meal. Much appreciated." I picked up my glass of orange juice and took a large swig. "But can we get down to it now? Because honestly, this 'you have a perfect life' schtick is kind of sad. I feel like I'm in a bottle episode of…well, pretty much any sci-fi or supernatural show made in the last fifty years. What's next? I wake up in an insane asylum and you try to convince me that my life in the occult was all just a delusion? You're better than this."

Rebecca smiled at me. "We are. But that's not what this is. We know you won't be fooled by any of this. That's not the intention."

Suddenly she was gone. Everything was gone, replaced by a large courtyard lined with columns and partial stone walls that lead out into endless night. Thirty yards in front of me were a line of robed figures sitting in a semi-circle of stone chairs and regarding me from behind intricately carved wooden masks. I recognized the wood as the same kind I used for the dolls, and I knew from reputation that the inside of the masks contained long spikes driven deep into the eye sockets of the wearers. I was finally before the Blind Court. God help me.

"Hey guys. Or girls. It's hard to tell with the…" I gestured to my face. "You know. So what's the intention then?"

One of the figures spoke, but sound carried weird in the courtyard, so it was hard to say who. The voice was feminine, but different than the mimicry of Rebecca. "To show you what you can have here if you cooperate. We don't want to kill you or torture you. We can do those things, of course, but you are much more useful to us alive and cooperative. And in exchange for your cooperation, we will grant you a wonderful life far better than the lonely and dangerous existence you've known up to this point."

The kitchen chair I was sitting on hadn't disappeared with the rest, but when I stood up now I saw it fade away swiftly. Interesting. "The problem is, I don't believe you. Not just because you're super-evil abras of the cadabras, but because you're already lying to me. Not the best first impression, ya'll."

A different, male voice spoke up this time. "Why do you

say that?"

I smiled at them, trying to keep my voice steady. "Because you can't torture or kill me, can you? Because of my…implants, your magic doesn't work on me. You can shape things around me like the fake house or this courtyard, but nothing can actually affect me because of the way your magic is designed. Can't have it touching outside infernal magic, huh?"

There was a heavy silence before the first voice spoke again. "You sewing tumerin coins under your skin was very clever, but ultimately pointless. While it does offer you some level of protection against us, what stops us from beating you, drugging you, ripping you apart slowly? More traditional means of harm are still available to us. You aren't as safe as you believe, dollmaker."

I stuck my hands in my pajama pants…I have to say, I really do enjoy pajama pants with pockets, and out of everything, I had to tip my hat to them on that. There are just so many uses for a pocket on sleepwear. And these weren't the little shitty pockets that you could put a couple of dimes in. You could put all kinds of stuff in it. Cellphones, remotes, the fork I had swiped from the table during breakfast…so many uses.

I pulled out the fork and held it up to them. "Let's just see." I drove the tines of the fork down into my leg, feeling relief as it crumbled apart upon hitting my leg. I looked back up at them. "That's what I figured. I can interact with things here, but nothing can actually penetrate me or harm me because it's all based on your magic. It's the same reason I felt safe eating your fake food…which was pretty fucking tasty, by the way. Compliments to the evil chef. The drugs they gave me before sending me over, those were normal, terrestrial drugs. But you don't have normal drugs here, do you? You don't have anything from other realms here, do you?"

"No, because you have to keep everything hermetically sealed here in your little panic room. Nothing new comes in except for people like me, I suppose, and even that is a big risk. Keeping this place going is a lot of work, isn't it? And if you introduce foreign elements, it makes it even harder to keep stable. I can't imagine what having multiple coins of Hell here must be like for you."

The male voice was back now. "You overstep, Westgate. You are before the Blind Court, in our own private realm. Our power was unparalleled on what you call the terrestrial realm, but here? Here we are God."

I could tell where the voice was coming from now because the masked figure third from the left was waving his fist as he boasted. It made it easier to direct my response as I smirked at him. "Are you now? Because to me you look like a bunch of frustrated, scared occultists that created a blood tesseract powered by enslaved demons to try and hide from the Hunter and the Hell that is waiting for you. Not a bad plan, all things considered. Until you were dumb enough to bring objects laden with outside infernal magic into your little sandbox. I wonder if the demons you have chained up in the basement can already smell the coins? I wonder what they would do if they got just one of them?"

Several members of the court were looking at each other, which seemed odd since they all were physically blind. Still, even magic sight falls back on mundane habits I suppose. Mr. Shaky Fist leaned forward in his chair.

"We are the rulers of this realm. You will submit or you and everything you hold dear will be destroyed."

I let the anger show in my voice this time. "To paraphrase a favorite movie of mine, it looks to me like you're rulers of Jack and Shit, and Jack's left town. As for threats, let's talk about who can take what from whom."

"Wait. So what's a blood tesseract?"

Abraham stopped and frowned at me. He was being helpful now, giving me information that might help me save Teddy, but he made a point with every word and movement of letting me know how much he resented it. We were sitting in a tidy living room on opposite ends of a large sofa, and I kept glancing around, trying to seem casual as I looked for any signs of danger. I knew Teddy trusted him, but I didn't, and the fact that he had demanded Heckle stay outside only made me more suspicious.

Still, so far so good. He had told me that the Blind Court was a Circle of very powerful occultists that had been at the top of the food chain when the Hunter had appeared in Hell. Once they saw the way the infernal wind was blowing, they had set to work putting an insurance policy in place by creating what Abraham called a blood tesseract.

"Basically, it's a magical pocket dimension. It's not a Realm like Hell or Incarnata, but instead its more like a soap bubble sustained by the magic and wills of those that create it. Inside there, they control everything. They can't die, they can alter reality, you name it. But that takes a lot of power. It is theorized it can be done with large-scale human sacrifice, but that is very inefficient, and constantly bringing new elements into the soap bubble can make it less stable. So this group figured out a way to enslave nine demons through special masks. The masks allow them to use the blood of the weakened demons to power the tesseract perpetually, or at least for several centuries at this point."

I nodded. "Ok. That makes sense, I guess. So you think that's where they took Teddy?"

He took another swig of the beer he had been nursing since I arrived. "Oh sure. No doubt. They won't risk leaving their special place and they'll want to deal with him personally I'd imagine. Problem is, there's very few ways of getting there unless they want to let you in."

"But there is a way?"

Abraham grimaced. "If you want to call something that will almost certainly kill you 'a way', then yeah." He leaned forward. "There are these contraptions called boxes of shadow. There are only a few of them, and they're all different in what they look like and how they work. They're very dangerous, but they can be useful in finding out certain information, like where Ted is." He puffed out a breath and caught my eyes. "I'm telling you though, he isn't worth this. Threats to me aside, you seem like a nice girl. You go fucking around with one of those boxes, it will probably kill you. If it doesn't, the next step or the Court will. Just leave all this behind. If you are inheriting all your uncle's shit, you can have yourself a real nice life somewhere far from all this stuff that you don't understand."

I felt my fists clenching on my lap, but I just gave him a smile. "Noted. But I'm not leaving him. So where can I find one of these boxes? And what's the next step after that?"

He sighed. "Well, I've never been fool enough to actually mess with one of the boxes of shadow, but I know a lady who used to have one. Runs a pawnshop last I heard. I can get you the address. As for the next step, you need to find an Incarnata."

I frowned. "That's a Realm, right?"

"It is, but it's also what you call things from that realm. Some creatures from Incarnata can travel between Realms and can come to our world as well. That can be for a variety of reasons, but its not uncommon for them to set themselves up as brokers of a sort. They will trade goods and services for a price. But again, that price isn't something you're going to want to pay, whatever it might be."

I waved my hand, unable to hide my irritation and

impatience any longer. "Yeah, yeah. I get it. Gloom and doom. Foreboding with a side of I told you so. So I can get one of these Incarnata to get me to where they're keeping Teddy?"

Abraham's expression was angry as he nodded. "In theory, yeah."

"Okay, cool. Where do I find one?"

"You don't."

The voice was coming from my right, and I let out a little scream as a figure suddenly appeared in front of us. It was Peter, Dilly's monstrous brother who hadn't attended the party where Teddy killed his sister and all her friends. He seemed more stooped than before, and I had the thought that his back must have healed back poorly in the time since Milly had flung him against that wall. But poor posture was the least of his problems. As before, he was a twisted ruin of a human being, the red worms that lived in his flesh working constantly across the shattered landscape of his face as he gave me his version of a smile.

"Long time no see, Cora. I was hoping to find Teddy myself, make him pay for all he's done, but this all sounds like too much work." The human side of his face gave a lopsided pout. "I guess you'll have to do."

Uncle Teddy and Cora: The Devil's Viewfinder

Imagine two 18-wheelers carrying full loads of toxic waste. They are at opposite ends of a two mile stretch of road, barreling towards each other as their engines whine and their wheels smoke in protest. Imagine them plunging headfirst toward each other, only the destruction of the other on their cold, metal minds.

Now imagine you are sitting on a raggedy couch between them.

The thing about magic is that it is entirely different than what you see in the movies or on t.v. Instead of lightning bolts and fireballs, you get a dead, unnatural silence that reminds me of the minutes before a sudden and terrible storm begins to roll in. Rather than glowing wizard staffs and billows of smoke, you get an oily residue that suffuses the air as it thickens with something malignant and wrong. That silence? That icky dirty feeling that makes your skin crawl and your teeth feel too big for your head? That's two opposing wills fueled by years of ritual, discipline, and dealings with inhuman creatures. They're revving their engines and peeling their tires as they slam against each other, and you can sense it, but you can't see it.

Instead, you see the monstrosity known as Peter staring down at the man known as Abraham McMillen. And if not for the weight of power you can feel burning through the oxygen in the room, it might look like the world's most intense staring contest. It might even be funny.

But then Abraham's eyes burst and he starts to scream.

Peter may not have been a match for his sister Dilly or

her friend Milly in the magic department, but it was clear he was no slouch. He had managed to follow me here and eavesdrop on my conversation with Abraham McMillen without detection, and whatever Abraham's knowledge and abilities, I could somehow sense that the thirty second invisible war between them wasn't going his way. That's why I ignored the itching sensation growing on my chest and eased the stun gun out of my jacket pocket, holding it ready as a last resort. I had little doubt Peter could rip me apart if I caught his attention too much, but if Abraham lost, I wasn't going down without a fight.

The problem with Peter, well…the relevant problem with Peter, at least…was that he was a sadist. When he had Abraham on the ropes, wailing and thrashing as his head started to cave in, he kept drinking it in, a twisted smile writhing contentedly on his ruined face like a snake trying to get comfortable on a sunny rock. So during the three seconds he was delighting in painfully killing the other occultist in the room, I jammed a lighting bolt into his weirdly spongey ribs.

He collapsed immediately, but I knew my time was limited. I had pulled the stun gun because I needed him to be instantly incapacitated. If he had time to speak or gesture after being shot or stabbed, I was most likely fucked. But the stun gun bought me a window, however short.

Still, I felt my heart thudding as I heard him trying to say something as he toppled to the ground. He wasn't even entirely human any more, so who knew how well electricity would even work on him? But rather than a spell, it sounded like he was trying to threaten or mock me.

"You…should…have killed me."

I was fully on my feet now, my other hand holding the small semi-automatic that I had tucked into my belt before coming to see Abraham. I could hear honest confusion in my voice as I leveled the gun at Peter before emptying it into his chest.

"Well yeah, of course. That's what I'm doing."

His body jumped from the impact of the bullets, and as I reached the end of the magazine I moved up to his head. He was still by the time I fired the last round, but I didn't want to take any chances. Looking back at Abraham, it was clear he was already dead, so I decided to see if a hunch I had was right.

"Heckle, come in here."

There was a loud crack as Heckle broke open the door and entered the room. When Abraham was alive, there were wards in place that kept most people out unless he invited them in, Peter obviously not included. Now that he was dead, however, his magics were gone too.

"Are you all right?" Heckle's voice was deep and gravelly, and while his face remained a relative blank, his tone actually seemed concerned.

I nodded and gave him a shaky smile. "Yeah. Just make sure this fucker is dead. Tear him up and watch both of them while I look for anything of use. We have to burn this place when we go."

Heckle nodded silently as he bent down and began casually dismembering Peter's body with his bare hands. Feeling my stomach turn over, I started searching for anything of use in the apartment, including on Abraham's ruined corpse. Tucked away in an old notebook, I found the address for a pawn shop and a note that said "Izu or Franklin Box of Shadows?", so I figured that was a good place to start. But I also needed to know where to find an Incarnata after finding the box. I searched for twenty minutes, my ears pricked for the sound of approaching sirens the entire time. But there was nothing. Finally giving up, I grabbed an armful of what looked like the most important books and papers Abraham had in his collection and handed it to Heckle.

I had run across a small bottle of lighter fluid under the kitchen sink and now I squirted it around the room, liberally dousing the two dead men before wiping off the gun and placing it in Abraham's hand. I knew it was sloppy, but I hoped the impending fire would make up for our lack of finesse. Striking a long kitchen match, I tossed it onto one of Teddy's only friends, if you could call him that. Within moments the living room was fully ablaze and we were heading down the back stairs and calling Jeckle to pick us up as sirens finally began to wail into earshot.

I breathed a sigh of relief. If I hadn't seen a sign of police coming by the time we reached the car, I was going to have to call it in myself. I didn't want to risk someone else getting hurt if the fire spread beyond Abraham's apartment, but it was better that I didn't have to be the one to make the call. As we got in, I glanced at Jeckle and he just nodded to me, his eyes placid. I'm not sure, but I think the two of them may have some kind of telepathic link. If I'm right, I guess he already knew everything that had happened anyway. Either way, my two magpie golems left me alone as I looked out at the passing scenery, my hands shaking as I tried not to cry.

****

"Hello? Is this Mr. Saltzmann?"

I felt my stomach fluttering as I waited for his reply. In the past few hours I had learned that the woman who potentially had a box of shadows had died and that her niece had inherited her pawn shop. I then found out that the niece had died too. My last hope was the niece's husband, and his voice was strange when he finally answered.

"Yes. I guess."

So far so good, even though he sounded like he was either stoned or had just been in a bad car accident. "Hi there.

My name is Cora Westgate. I've been trying to track you down. Or at least something I think you have." I sat there, waiting for a response, but no dice. "It's a box. It's called an…Izu Box of Shadows, I think?"

Another pause, and I almost threw out "Franklin Box of Shadows" as an alternative, but then he was speaking again.

"Why do you want it?"

I felt a surge of relief. "So you do have it. Awesome. Look, my uncle…he's been abducted. By very bad people. And I think the box can help me find him. I know that sounds crazy, but if…"

"Fine."

Something in the back of my head warned this was coming way too easy, but I didn't have the luxury of questioning it. Every minute I wasted was longer that Teddy was stuck in…well, I wasn't sure what, but I doubted it was good. "Oh, wow. Great! Look, I have your address and I can be there in two hours if that's okay. I'll be glad to pay you well for it but…"

"No, I won't be here when you get here. Just take it."

I went to thank him, and to ask if he was okay. He just sounded so…lost. But the line was already dead. I reached his house in the middle of the night, and when I knocked, the door just swung open. As I entered, I could smell the sharp copper scent of blood in the air. Pausing at the threshold, I poked my head in further and saw where the smell was coming from. There were two dead men and a dead woman in the living room. It was hard to tell, but it seemed like one of the men had killed the others with a knife before turning it on himself. But before that, he had written a letter.

It was sitting on top of the box in the center of the room, the yellow paper stiff in spots with freshly dried blood. The box itself was pristine and beautiful in a vaguely sinister way, with its black wood and smoky gray metal seeming to radiate a mild inner warmth. I saw a metal cylinder in the middle of the contraption and what appeared to be small slots on each of its six sides. Leaving the box alone for the moment, I turned back to the yellow paper. It was a letter to me, at least mostly. It warned me to leave the box alone, or destroy it if I could. I guess it was the last thing he did before he killed himself.

I hesitated after reading it. I had little doubt the box was responsible or at least connected to all the death laying around me, and I could feel the weight of Saltzmann's words. Words he had spent his last living moments writing in an attempt to keep me from repeating his own mistakes. Warning me that the box wanted me to take it. That it knew that I would, despite his plea.

The thing was, I had no other options to help Teddy. I felt like I was on a massive game board, jumping my piece from square to square as I worked my way toward wherever Teddy was being held. Find the devil pig. Talk to Abraham. Find the evil box that probably killed these people. Every step brought me closer to getting Teddy back in theory, but I had no real way of knowing if I was making progress. All I could do was keep pushing on until I got him back or knew that I couldn't.

But if I failed, it wasn't going to be because I gave up or chickened out. I touched the tumerin around my neck as I approached the box again. I had started wearing it most of the time since Teddy was taken despite his prior warnings of the dangers it could pose. It had protected me before, and besides, Teddy had given it to me. It made me feel a bit like he was with me.

I found another note discarded on the floor near the box and picked it up. It was instructions on how to use the box. Following the instructions, I removed the collection of possessions already in the central chamber and placed a silver ring my mother had given me inside. Then I spun the tube and looked through the closest slot, holding the idea of finding Teddy firmly in my mind.

The sensation of being somewhere else overtook me immediately. I heard a hushed voice whispering to me in some unknown language, its words feeling like worms trying to eat their way deep into my brain. At the same time, I was seeing…or being transported to…several different scenes.

The first was a small town I didn't recognize. I didn't see any people, but in the distance I saw a sign that read "Welcome to Brimley!" I took a few steps toward what looked like a nearby truck stop, but then I was gone. Now I was in the forests of Hell. I couldn't be sure, but I thought it was near where I had last left it, the same waterfall faintly audible over the buzzing voice pressing ever closer to me. I felt a surge of fear. Viewing something through the box was akin to being in a dream that you only partially realize is a dream. The reality of what I was seeing was constantly warring with my dim recognition of the fact that I was actually in that poor man's living room and not running my hand over the rough and icy bark of one of the skeletal trees filling my vision.

Then I was in a new place. This was a courtyard of some kind, though it had the feeling of something that was staged to invoke awe and fear more than something that was used for more…courtyardy things. I don't really know what you do in a courtyard, but you get my drift. It was weird and creepy, but also somehow phony feeling. And I wasn't sure how any of this was getting me closer to…

"Teddy!" I blurted it out before I could stop myself. Further down the courtyard there were a group of figures seated on stone chairs, but standing a bit closer I could make out the back of my uncle. I tried to run to him in my vison form, knowing in the back of my head that it wouldn't work, and while I did seem to travel toward him, I was suddenly somewhere else again.

It was a rundown park of some kind in what looked like a shabby part of a normal city. I was disappointed I had lost sight of Teddy, but I could tell this place was important. It was where I needed to go next. The voice in my head was almost unbearable now, but I forced myself to focus as I looked around for any clues as to where I was at or what this place was called. After a moment I saw a small rusty sign dangling from the side of a lopsided chain link fence. I was trying to read it when I felt my chest grow hot and itchy where the tumerin was resting. Then everything faded away and I found myself back in the blood-soaked living room.

I was frustrated, but I couldn't help but feel relief when I realized the voice was gone too. Touching the coin around my neck, I could tell it was still warm. Maybe it had protected me from the box after all. Either way, I needed to get the thing loaded in my car and get going. Standing up shakily, I said the name that had been on the rusty sign, testing it on my tongue to make sure it sounded right and was seated firmly in my memory.

"Amerson Park."

I'm not sure what's waiting for me there, but I have a feeling it's nothing good.

Uncle Teddy and Cora: Dealing with the Debbil

"Do you have somethin' ta offer?"

I was standing in a bright patch of afternoon sun, but it felt like the whole world was cloudy and gray as I looked at the creature that had asked me the question. It was…Well, I don't know what it was, really. Just looking at it, I'd describe it as a large homeless man made out of garbage and decay, full of dirt and trash and dead things.

But it was more than that too. Its green eyes of broken glass flashed with intelligence, and when its silver hypodermic teeth parted, the words that slipped between them were rough but knowing. I think it was that dry, almost business-like tone that made looking up at it worse. It drove home the point that I was the interloper here, not it. It knew what was going on, what the rules were, what its role was. I was traveling purely off a combination of Abraham's shoddy notes, educated guesses, and a determination to not give up on getting Teddy back.

It would have to be enough. Stepping forward, I met its iridescent gaze and nodded. "I see you well, Incarnata, and I am here with both an offer and the fervent hope that a deal can be struck."

Its large, shifting head returned my nod as it spoke. "Well-spoken. The dealing has begun."

****

(From the notes of Abraham McMillen-partially paraphrased so they make fucking sense)

Incarnata: The name given to one of the Seven Realms. Also the general name for all beings that originate from there.

The realm Incarnata is a highly dangerous place, and was generally considered riskier to visit than infernal Hell so long as one had an escape route planned from Lucifer's Realm. The Hunter's invasion and slow conquering of Hell has increased that Realm's dangerousness greatly, but Incarnata still remains a very dicey proposition as well.

The reason it remains a goal for so many is because of what all it can offer. The Incarnata Realm is one born almost entirely out of belief and willpower, ideas and dreams. While it is highly mutable and wildly unpredictable, there are also many indications that it can be a source of great power and fulfillment.

(Two **paragraphs** are scratched out here so thoroughly that I couldn't make out anything other than a handful of words: "*tulpa*", "*well*", and "*Elder*" in the first paragraph and "*Imago*" and "*Halloween Room*" in the second.)

These incredible displays of power aren't limited to within their own Realm, however. Many Incarnata settle in our reality or in others. There are accounts of Incarnata living relatively mundane lives on the terrestrial plane, while other stories tell of those that cultivate power through becoming a legend or myth. It's hard to know what is true and what is bullshit.

But what is known for sure is that some Incarnata are here with a specific job or purpose. They act as ferrymen for people that want to cross from one realm to another. Brokers for certain hard to find objects obtained from places most can't go. While that all sounds great, the price is usually very high. Unlike demons, an Incarnata isn't interested in your soul. But they find pleasure and power in acquiring something you value greatly, whatever that may be. Incarnatas are allegedly always truthful, but that doesn't stop them from being shrewd dealmakers. I've heard it said that the only people that deal with Incarnatas are those that want to lose more than they gain. Or as my friend Chester used to say, dealing with an Incarnata is a lot like going to an orgy at a power tool convention. You always get screwed in a weird way and you'll likely leave without all your parts.

****

I tugged up the shoulder straps of the backpack I was wearing as I considered what I had learned from both Abraham and his notes. The backpack was weighted down with all the tumerin from the devil piggy bank, and I knew that the infernal currency was very valuable in some circles, no pun intended. But looking into the Incarnata's glittering eyes, I didn't think money would be of any interest to him.

That opening response to his question about "did I have something to offer" had come from another of Abraham's notes, and while it seemed to please the creature, I wasn't sure what the best follow-up was. I didn't want to offer the wrong thing and piss it off, but I also didn't want to offer more than needed to get what I wanted. Sensing a growing impatience, I forced myself to begin.

"What do I have that is of value to you?"

The Incarnata shifted slightly on its oozing feet before giving an almost humanlike shrug. "How am I ta know what you got and don't got? Am I your kin or keeper?"

It was hard to tell, but it sounded irritated now. Its metal teeth rasped together to make a low, unpleasant ringing sound that seemed to echo through the stillness of the abandoned park. For the fiftieth time I wondered if not bringing Heckle and Jeckle with me had been the right call. They were great guards, but I didn't know how their presence might unnecessarily complicate things with the Incarnata—I didn't need brute force, I needed an agreement. I also needed to approach this differently, and fast. So I tried it from the other end.

"I need you to get my uncle, Theodore Westgate, from

the blood tesseract controlled by the Blind Court. I will pay…what is fair and reasonable for that."

A dry, rustling sound that I took as laughter issued from the creature. "Ain't dealin' with him. Dealing with you, ain't I? So if you need travelin' it'll be you that does it."

I nodded, my heart sinking slightly that the simple, easy way wasn't going to work. "Can you get me to where Uncle Teddy is and bring us both back out of there once I find him?"

There was a pause before he nodded. "I suppose so — if you're touching when I bring you back. But I can't see well in that place, so the return will be at a set time, not whenever you like." He sent out a green tendril of tongue that looked like a slimy, dying vine, its multitude of pulsating branches caressing the spaces between those needle teeth before retreating back into the dark, rotten muck inside. "But what do you have ta offer for such as that? Travels such as these aren't undertaken lightly or without great expense." It teased out the last words as though it savored the taste of them, and I felt my heart thudding faster as I realized I was no closer to knowing what I should offer.

Sucking in a breath, I tried to feel my way forward. "I don't know much about you, but I think I'm right that you don't care anything about money or mundane wealth. Maybe even offering such as that would be an insult."

The Incarnata's eyes flashed with an inner light that made my chest tighten with fear. "You would be correct. On both counts."

I could feel myself on the edge. If I didn't give a satisfactory response now, I thought the dealing might be over, and it seemed unlikely that would go well for me. My mind raced back over what I had learned from Abraham about Incarnata and what the creature had said and done. Maybe somewhere in there…

"My family." I blurted out. "My parents. They're both dead now, and the memory of them is all I have left. I loved them very much." I felt tears springing to my eyes, the enormity of what I was about to offer settling on my heart like a weighted shroud. "I offer my memories of my mother and father to you in exchange for safe passage to where my uncle Teddy is located, as well as safe passage back to this world fifteen minutes later for both of us."

The creature raised a single finger that seemed comprised of a candy bar wrapper intertwined with black clay and crawling beetles. "If you are touching him when I return you to this world."

I nodded. "Yes. If I am touching him when you go to return us to this world."

Giving me a gruesome, silvery smile, he took a step forward. "The deal is struck." Without warning, his hand shot forward and gripped my head, the feeling of cold, squirming earth against my forehead pushing an involuntary gasp from my mouth a moment before my jaws clenched tight. I felt him in my head, pillaging quickly but roughly as he looked for the memories of my parents. Within a few seconds, I felt a terrible coolness seeping through my brain as something precious was taken from me. I was crying freely now, because while I knew I'd had parents and remembered my deal with the Incarnata a moment before, I couldn't call up any specific memory of either of my parents any more. They were just gone.

The Incarnata released my head and I stepped back, cradling my face in my hands. I was sobbing quietly enough that I could still hear a soft popping sound to my left as something in the park changed. Looking up, I saw there was now a small wooden door standing freely a few feet away. I glanced back at the creature and it nodded.

"Fairly paid. Now go. You have fifteen minutes."

****

My negotiations with the Blind Court had broken down fairly quickly. They were unable to do more than contain me and offer mild irritations because of the tumerin under my skin, and I was going to give Cora a bit more time before I went to Plan B. So what I was left with was temporary exile to a bare white room that was completely empty except for an uncomfortable recliner that squeaked shrilly at every movement.

The great Blind Court had decided they would force my compliance through boredom.

It wasn't a terrible plan. Their thought was that being trapped here with them, I'd eventually give in and work with them when I saw the alternative was an eternity of mind-numbing blahness. I would like to say I could just last forever in some zen-like state of internal peace, but fuck that. And besides, my DVR only holds so much. Papa needs to get home.

Still, I tried to be patient. Cora would likely come through, and Plan B wasn't a good option unless there was no other option. So I just had to get my mind on something…

"Teddy!"

I turned around in the chair as it let out a terrible squeal. Cora was in the room with me, looking a strange combination of ecstatic, sad, and terrified. She also had a gross glob of mud or dog shit or something on her head. I bore it in mind as I jumped up and went to give her a hug, carefully avoiding the earthworm that was delicately exploring her bangs.

"Who has the best niece? I do!" Pulling back, I looked at her more seriously. "Are you okay? Did you have any problems getting here?"

She let out a tired laugh as she picked the worm from her hair and flung it toward the chair. "You could say that. But

I made it. And we're getting pulled back out in less than fifteen minutes, so we have to be in physical contact when that happens."

I frowned at her. "Fifteen minutes? From when?"

"About thirty seconds ago, I think. The Incarnata didn't have a stopwatch or anything."

I felt my skin go cold. "Incarnata? So you wound up having to deal with one? Abraham didn't have another way?"

She shook her head. "If he did, he didn't tell me before Milly's brother, Peter, showed up and killed him."

I frowned and wanted to ask more questions about that, but it would have to wait. "Did it say if it was fifteen minutes on the terrestrial plane or here?"

A new look of worry spread across her face. "Oh God. I don't know. It all happened fast and I forgot to ask. Is time a lot different here?"

I raised an eyebrow. "I don't know. How long have I been gone?"

"Um, about six weeks."

Rubbing my chin, I nodded thoughtfully. "It's as I feared then. Time is much slower here, as I have been here for twenty-five years by my best estimate."

Cora's eyes widened as she took a step back. "So we might be here for weeks or months?"

Grinning at her, I shook my head. "Nah, just fucking with you. I think time is the same now. Used to be different maybe, but my devil coins have been messing with their mojo a bit." I ducked out of the way as she swung at me, but I was too slow. Pain exploded in my ear as I backed away. "Shit! Sorry! Sorry! Truce!" Holding up my hands, I looked up and saw her smiling at me.

"I'm glad I found you, asshole."

I gave her another quick hug, blinking quickly until my vision wasn't so watery. "Me too, Cora. It means more to me than you know." Pulling away again, I frowned at her. "And I want to talk more about your dealings with that Incarnata. But for now, there's no time. Did you bring the tumerin from the piggy bank?"

She slung the backpack off into my arms and I grunted at the weight. "Good job. This should work."

Cora raised an eyebrow. "What are they for exactly? I mean how do they help us here? Just destabilize the place? We're going to be leaving soon anyway."

I grabbed the backpack by the shoulder straps and swung it like an oversized mace at the closest blank wall. The bag tore the wall apart like tissue paper. Pointing at the hole, I explained. "This many tumerin can do a lot more than just keep them from directly fucking with us or make their blood tesseract rumbly in its tumbly. We can shatter constructs like this wall, for instance." Glancing out, I saw the hole opened out onto a dark hallway. Beckoning for her to follow, I went on. "It also expands the range that their magic won't work on us, making it difficult for them to trick us or keep us lost or trapped."

We were walking down the hall now, and I stopped at a door marked "Boiler Room". I pointed at the sign. "Now I would lay money that either one of these dweebs is a Freddy Kruger fan or…wait, they didn't even have boiler rooms when these fossils were making this place. Freddy fan it is." I paused, the corners of my mouth drooping a little. "See? That makes me a bit sad. I feel like with more time, we could have found understanding by bonding over our mutual love of Robert Englund's body of work." I sighed. "But such is life. Now let's go free the demons so they can murder these douchebags."

The scary boiler room is a common horror movie trope, and with good reason. It's dark, confusing, and full of hot pipes and eerie noises. Just kind of naturally unsettling. But you know what is more unsettling? A giant stone basement filled with chained up demons.

I had only seen true demons once before, and that was in Hell when I was running from the Hunter. I had been terrified then too, but the sad sack demons (horrifying as they were) that I saw there were really just another line item on my fear to-do-list at the time. Now though, they had my full attention.

There were small demons, large demons. Some looked human or at least humanish, while others looked like a snake and a spider had a baby with taffy. And not normal taffy either, but very evil taffy. I had expected them to talk to us, or scream threats, or maybe howl like a monster. Instead, they all sat silently staring at us as we entered, each one of them bound by silver chains and secured to devices that bled them endlessly, sending channels of black blood away into small holes in the basement walls. Suppressing a shiver, I leaned toward Teddy.

"I think I know what you're planning, but are you sure it's a good idea?"

He turned and looked at me with a smile, but his eyes were hard. "A good idea? That's debatable. But they fucked with us. People don't get to fuck with us and live." He tipped me a wink. "Got to keep up our rep and all." He turned back to the demon horde chained up before us. The closest one looked kind of like a giant beagle except more…runny. "And besides, these guys aren't dumb. They know who put them here, and they know they have to work fast once they're free to get the Blind Court before they skitter away. Right guys?"

In creepy unison, they all gave a single curt nod.

"Cool beans." With that, he unzipped the backpack and started tossing out tumerin like chicken feed as we walked down the center of the long, dark room. I was very aware of keeping my hand on his shoulder just in case we got pulled back early, but I couldn't help but watch as the demons began scrabbling for the coins they could reach. With each one they touched, you could almost see them regaining their strength, and by the time we reached the far end of the room, I was already hearing the first of the chains snap.

I put my back to the far wall, half-expecting that the demons were going to turn on us instead of heading for the exit. But for the most part, they didn't even spare us a backward glance. The one exception was a smaller demon that looked like a badly burned child. It took a tentative step towards us, but then stopped. Eyes widening, it spun around and ran after the rest.

I looked at Teddy. "What was that about?"

He shrugged. "Demons are notorious for being…"

There was a disorienting rush of images and suddenly we were back in our world.

"…weird fuckers." Teddy finished. Glancing around, he gave a frown. "Where are we?"

I was taking in our surroundings as well, and while I wasn't sure, I thought I recognized the truck stop down the street. "I think we're in a town called Brimley."

Teddy was about to ask something else when we saw a man chasing a woman down the street. They were both moving very fast, but he was clearly faster, and as we watched, he slammed into her back and sent her skidding twenty feet across the asphalt before she came to a bloody halt.

"Why are you doing thif, Evening tar? We wanted you to lead uf all to the new glory! But you're no different than him!

You're just another forry excuse of a Debbil...." The words came out loose and half-formed from her bloody lips, ending in a wet, barely articulated whine as the man stomped on her head hard enough to send a thick, red spray across the street in our direction. That's when he looked up and saw us.

"More? How many demons are there in this town?" The man was already stalking towards us when I heard Teddy let out a groan.

"Fuck. Fucking Brimley." I glanced his way, but he was already stepping forward, putting himself between me and the man. "Look, we're not demons and we have no..."

The man was suddenly a blur, moving past Teddy and then to me. I felt a flash of pain followed by rocky ground biting into my bare skin. Because I was naked.

I looked around, suppressing a shiver as the icy air of my new surroundings soaked into me. I was in the middle of freezing darkness punctuated by the stark forests of the new Hell.

"Oh no."

Tick Head

When my brother Sidney was four years old, he was possessed by a demon. I wasn't even born yet, but I've heard the stories. The way my mama always told it, it all started when a friend of hers gave Sidney a stuffed rabbit named Mr. Jinkies. It had belonged to the woman since she herself was a child, and was given to Sidney to help with nightmares he was having, as the same toy had helped the woman's night terrors when she was young as well.

At first, Sidney had improved. But then my parents noticed that he was acting different. Anger and violence were part of it, but that wasn't the worst. No, the thing that always upset Mama when she talked about it was that he would get this terrible sly look on his face when he thought no one was looking. It was an adult look, an evil look, that didn't belong on the face of any child, much less Sidney, who had always been sweet and kind.

It only got worse over the next several years. I was born when Sidney was six, and I remember things when they were at their worst. Strange things would happen around the house. We were all plagued by strange and terrible dreams. And any time we had a pet, they would die mysteriously. The unspoken question was never whether Sidney had a hand in it, but rather whether he had physically killed the poor thing or had it been done by the unseen creature that haunted his heart?

For a long time, we didn't have a name for that creature, and it wasn't until later we started to refer to it as Mr. Jinkies. This was partly because giving it a name would have meant acknowledging it was real. Beyond that, Mr. Jinkies was the name of the stuffed rabbit, and for the first few years, no one even made the connection between the toy and the entity that had taken hold of Sidney. The work friend that had given us the rabbit had left mama's office and moved away soon after we got Mr. Jinkies, but at the time no one realized that Sidney's odd behavior and fixation on the toy was anything other than him acting up and loving Mr. Jinkies.

And then one day, the rabbit just disappeared. I was an infant at the time, but my father told me once that the strangest thing about it going missing was that Sidney didn't seem to care. He had been inseparable from that thing since he first had gotten it, but when it was gone, my brother didn't miss a beat.

It wasn't until later that we understood that was because the real Mr. Jinkies had never left.

****

I never knew my brother when he wasn't possessed, so at first it didn't seem strange when he would say cruel things to me or hurt me when no one was around. As I got older and saw how other children were, how other siblings treated each other, I realized my mistake. I told our parents, and they were properly upset, but I can't say they were entirely surprised. They had already figured out something was deeply wrong with Sidney by that point, and if they weren't ready to say words like "spirit" or "demon" yet, they should have known enough to watch him more closely around his little brother.

Still, if I hated them a little for their past willful blindness, I was relieved when his treatment of me became the breaking point. Before my outcry, Sidney had occasionally gone to child psychologists and medical doctors, but our parents had largely tried to handle his "condition" on their own. Looking back at it now that I'm older, I realize that this mainly consisted of them lying to each other, trading reassurances that this was all just a "phase" Sidney was going through.

But when they found out he had been hurting me, they sent him for in-house psychological evaluation and treatment. This was when I was about five and the more obvious strange things hadn't really started yet. But even if they had, my parents wouldn't have told the doctors about it. It was a double-edged shame, you see. A shame to have a child that was under the influence of some unseen, inhuman thing. And a shame to believe that something so foolish as that could be true.

So they wasted years on drugs and therapy. Punishments and pleading. And over the years, our house became a prison. My door was locked and there was a door wedge tight against the bottom. My parents' door was the same. Sidney's was similar, except his locked and wedged from the outside.

I used to lay in bed at night when I was a little boy, afraid to go to sleep because I didn't want to be taken by Sidney or the thing that lived behind his eyes. I knew he should be secure in his room—the door was heavy and solid, and there was chicken wire over the nailed down windows—but it didn't matter. I didn't think he necessarily needed to leave his room to hurt us. I could feel him—feel it—on the other side of the house. Thinking about us, sending out tendrils to poison us and weaken us, all while smiling that terrible knowing smile.

And week after month after year, it was working.

****

We grew weak from the constant exhaustion of being watchful. Of being worried and afraid. That's how it wins, you see. By being patient. It chips at you and chips at you, digging away at the walls of your sanity and your soul with a tiny little spoon, like in those prison escape movies where they tunnel out of their cell. And Mr. Jinkies was trying to get in, not out, but the reasoning was the same.

Just dig away a little at a time and no one will notice until it's too late.

I grew into a frightened, distrustful boy that was prone to anxiety and emotional outbursts. My father became increasingly short-tempered and would fly into terrible rages for no apparent reason. My mama took to over-medicating and crying almost daily. And all that time, Sidney would just sit back and watch, drinking it all in.

By the time I turned seven and Sidney was thirteen, it had become clear that our house was not really ours any more. We were seeing and hearing things, finding objects moved around, and living with the constant feeling that something was present that hated us and meant us harm. All of these things were frightening, and not just because of the events themselves, but because of the message they were meant to send. Mr. Jinkies was in control now. And the time for hiding was over.

You may be questioning why it took so long for my family to realize the depth of the problem we were facing. You have to understand that these kinds of things...they don't happen quickly. It's not like you see in a horror movie, where there's a big dramatic reveal full of blood on the walls and people levitating. Instead it's like a slow-moving virus infecting the person—and by extension, their family—and not making itself known until it is too late.

Except that's not quite right. Because Mr. Jinkies wasn't a virus. It was a parasite, draining all the love and goodness from Sidney and replacing it with something dark and filthy. Corrupting him and poisoning us all.

One day, my parents found where Sidney was preparing for some kind of...well, ritual I guess. They would never say what exactly they found, only that it was in the back of the old backyard work shed and it was terrible. And we never knew what the ritual was for. They couldn't even say for sure that it hadn't already been completed.

Sidney was questioned about it, of course, but he just smirked and acted ignorant. When he was younger, he would cry and act confused about how he was being treated — always the prime suspect when something went wrong and always locked away in his room at night. As he had gotten older, Sidney had become more openly hostile, full of contempt as he mocked our fear. Still, his expression changed that evening when there was a knock on the door.

The thin-faced man introduced himself as Christopher Darrow. A former priest, he said he now helped families in need of parapsychological counseling and assistance in some forms of what he called "spiritual warfare". He had a severe look about him, but he spoke with a kind of refined intelligence and authority that wasn't unkind. It was also clear from the beginning that my parents were desperate enough to take any help someone offered, particularly from someone that would actually believe what was going on.

There was still the sticking point of how Darrow knew to come there, however. That, he explained, was because he had contacts at several occult shops across the state. Sidney had apparently gone into a local one a few days ago when he was supposed to be in school. The shop owner had alerted Darrow about the visit immediately — both because of the dangerousness of the items Sidney had been inquiring about and the shop owner's intuition that the boy before him was infested by something unnatural.

Darrow was standing in our front hall by this point, and I was already seeing our parents' shoulders slump with relief. They were satisfied with the explanation and were more than willing to have him come examine Sidney. My brother was locked up in his room at this point, and Mama stayed with me as our father took the man upstairs. It wasn't long before I heard Sidney start to screech and yell, and in less than an hour, it was done.

My father was pale and clearly shaken by the experience, but he also seemed convinced that Darrow had expelled whatever was living in my brother for good. Darrow cautioned that it would be a slow process of recovery and that we would need to be patient with Sidney, but that we should see no further problems of the spiritual variety out of the boy.

And just like that, the man was gone again. It all happened so fast, and it wasn't until a few hours had passed that our parents started questioning the strangeness of the entire encounter. And honestly, they never questioned it too much, mainly because the man seemed to have worked a miracle.

Sidney was still odd acting for the next few days, but more because he just seemed subdued and traumatized. By the end of the month, he was like a different person. He was being nice to me, getting along with our parents, and not getting into trouble at school. By the time he was fourteen, the locks had come off our bedroom doors and our house felt like a home again.

In the ten years since, Sidney's completed high school and college with good grades. He's already been accepted into a philosophy graduate program that starts next spring. He was going to start this past fall, but then Mama suddenly got sick. We were thinking she was going to get over it—she had started feeling and looking better, after all—but then one day I came home from school to find out she had died thirty minutes before.

When Sidney was alone with her.

****

I remember the summer I spent with my uncle when I was ten. Things were good at home by then, but I still enjoyed being out in the world and away from all the memories our house held for a few days or weeks when I got the chance. My uncle's place was entirely different than anything I'd ever known — a remote farm surrounded by woods, it was peaceful and beautiful, free of fear or worry.

I used to spend hours walking in the nearby woods, and one day when I came back to the house, my uncle stopped me as I was walking in. I had a tick on my neck. I think my uncle expected I was going to be upset about it, but I had been through much worse than getting bit by a bug. Still, he cautioned me not to move as he got ready to remove it with a pair of needle-nose pliers.

The trick, he said, was to make sure you got the whole thing when you pulled it. If you didn't get close enough to the skin, you could pull off the body of the tick and leave the head. That, he said, could lead to an infection down the line. Almost as though he was disappointed I wasn't more squeamish about it, he went on, his mouth twitching with a barely suppressed mischievous grin. He told me he had even heard stories of the tick surviving without its body. Sometimes, he said, the tick head would just keep on living and drinking from its victim. Even at ten I knew he was joking, but I always remembered the story. I think even then I knew he was unintentionally teaching me something important.

****

Everyone thinks that Sidney is fine. Our father will hear no bad word spoken about him — when I asked why Sidney was with Mama when she died, our father told me he had allowed it. That Sidney said he had something important to tell her and that he had been right outside the door the entire time my brother was in there with her. That there wasn't anything mysterious or sinister about her death, she had just been sicker than anyone realized.

When I subtly ask Sidney's friends how he's been acting

lately, they act like I'm the weird one. They say he's been the same as always—awesome. I tried talking to his girlfriend about it, and at first she just looked confused. When I kept pressing, feeling sure she must have seen some sign of his wrongness, she started shaking her head and stood up to walk away. She said I was making her uncomfortable. I wanted to shout at her, to tell her that she should be fucking uncomfortable, because she was with a monster. But I held my tongue and told her I was sorry, that it was all just a bad joke on my part.

But, of course, it's not a joke. Mr. Jinkies is still in my brother just like always. Whatever that Darrow man did, at most he weakened it. He might have gotten the body of the tick. But he somehow left the head, and that's all that thing needs to live and control my brother. To make him kill our mother and corrupt our lives.

So this morning, I killed Sidney.

It wasn't difficult. He had always pretended to love me and trust me since he was "cured", and when I said I wanted to go out to our uncle's farm, he acted happy to come with me. It was our farm now, anyway. Our uncle had died at the end of that same summer where he told me about the tick head, and while we didn't get out there often, I still tried to go for walks in those woods every month or two.

I waited until we were near the edge of a tall cliff far back in the woods, one with a small but fast river rushing past some forty feet below. I struck him from behind with a rock, hoping the force of it would send him forward and off the edge. Instead, he wheeled backwards before falling down in the grass.

I had hit him in the back of the head, but clearly his brain was damaged some from the blow. He looked around confusedly, his right eye nearly black from its enlarged iris while his left eye fought to focus in on me. I thought he might curse me or try to attack, but instead he just sat there holding his head and crying.

"You have...have to fight it, Brian. I know it's in you. I've suspected it...for a long time...Just...don't...let it trick...you..." I was approaching him as he spoke, the sharp rock raised above my head. Seeming to understand that his words were having no effect, he stopped and lowered his eyes. "Please...don't hurt anyone els..."

After I was done, I threw him off the cliff and into the water below. As I suspected, the current quickly carried him downriver into a series of sharp rocks that would help conceal his initial injuries. My story would be that we had taken separate paths while walking, and when I couldn't find him after some time, I started searching for him. I'd been careful not to get any blood on me, and the rock was disposed of far away, so there is nothing to tie me to his death when they eventually find his body.

Besides, I doubted anyone was going to look into it that far anyway. He was a troubled boy, after all. Sure, he'd had a few good years, but who knew what demons he still harbored? Maybe he had committed suicide or maybe it was a tragic accident, but one thing was certain. His good younger brother would never have hurt him. Everyone knows what a good and caring guy I am. Always honest and thoughtful, never in trouble, graduating valedictorian in the fall. I have a sterling reputation.

I've made sure of it.

The only sad thing is that no one will appreciate the sacrifice I had to make in killing my own brother. They'll never know the evil that I've purged from this world by doing what they were too weak or selfish to do. They'll never realize I'm a hero.

But I guess that's okay. I didn't do it for the glory, and who knows, it may not be the last time I get to do something brave. Besides, I'm not stupid. I understand most people would think I murdered my brother rather than saving him and the world from a terrible monster. Those people can't accept a world that bleeds outside the mundane boundaries of their narrow view of things. They don't have the courage to see me as I am yet. But that's all right.

I'm very patient.

Uncle Teddy and Cora: Fucking Brimley

When the demon-killing, superhero asshole hit me, it hurt a good bit. Kind of like I would imagine getting shot wearing a bulletproof vest. The fact that it was meant to cave my chest in wasn't lost on me in retrospect, but the dull, aching shock of concussion and pain distracted me for a moment.

That moment was all he needed to zip over and rip out Cora's throat.

I felt rage filling me as I saw her gushing body topple to the ground like a lifeless doll. I didn't have time for that kind of anger now though. While the protections I'd already put in place had cushioned the attack and robbed it of any physical inertia (hence why I was still standing instead flying back like I was in a bad martial arts movie), the attack was only partly physical. If he got his hands on me and went to work, he could very well kill me before I was ready to die.

Raising my hands and trying to force a friendly smile, I called out to him as he rounded on me, his eyes widening when he saw I wasn't lying in a dead, ruined heap. "Hey, chief. Not a demon. Neither was that girl you just fucking murdered." I could feel the anger lapping against the boundaries of my control, and I tried to push it down again.

"Bullshit. That's all this town is. Just a nest of fucking demons."

Nodding, I tried smiling again. "No argument there. Brimley is a giant shithole. Wall to wall demons running from the new management in Hell. I'm sure you're doing God's work with your whole killing spree thing you've got going on here." I gestured to the dead demon he'd killed just moments before. "But we are not demons. We just got here."

The man stared at me for a moment, seeming to consider my words. "Then why are you here? And how do know about demons and this town and all?"

I puffed out my breath as I weighed both my options and how much truth I should give him. He seemed willing to talk, but that could be a bluff. And I thought I could delay him enough to do what I needed to do, but it would be a near thing. If I could get him to cooperate, or at least not try to murder me for five minutes, that would be better.

So some honesty then. We'll call it diet honesty. Same great honesty taste, but not so filling.

"Well, we got sent here by a…well, a magic creature is the simple answer. A magic creature that is apparently a giant dick and thought it would be funny to stick us in a place filled with demons. And I know about this stuff because demons and the people they run with have ruined my life since I was around your age. So I know a lot, but believe me, I'm not a fan."

He frowned at that. "Okay. But if that's true…if you're not a demon or at least buddies with them, why can I smell the corruption on you? I can almost see it."

Ugh. "Well, two reasons. First, like I said, I've been dealing with these people for decades, so no doubt, some of their stink has rubbed off on me. Second, I have a variety of things from Hell in my body at the moment, for reasons I don't have time to explain right now. But again, not your enemy, not a bad guy. Just need to get going so I can save the girl you just killed."

He raised an eyebrow, looking uncertain. "Save her? What do you mean? She's dead."

Gritting my teeth, I started judging the distance to the truck stop as I kept talking. "Look. What's your name? Mine's Teddy."

"Um, Phil."

"Okay Phil. Good to meet you. That woman you just killed is my niece, Cora. One of the best people I've ever known. Because of helping me, if she dies, she goes to Hell. Because of you, that's exactly where she is right now. With all the demons you just sent back there. And I have to get her out, right now, before something even worse finds her."

I could see that I was losing him as I talked. Aside from being covered in layers of drying blood, he looked like an average, nice-enough dude. Until his eyes started to flare with whatever weird bloodlust he had going on. I didn't know exactly what he was, but I had a strong feeling he was what a lot of the Infernals called "Vesper", their supposed anti-Hunter secret weapon that was going to reclaim Hell for them.

Well, it looked like they fucked that one up pretty good.

Still, whatever this guy really was or was headed towards being, he clearly didn't have a good grasp on much of anything, including his own impulse control. I half-expected him to bolt forward and try to kill me again when I said Cora was in Hell, but either way, I was past wasting time trying to placate Phil the Devil Messiah.

"Korscchulughtap."

Phil blinked. That was a bad sign already. According to what I read, that should bind someone from moving at all for at least a week. But given how he was shitting on demons like they were porta-potties at a chili cookoff, I had to account for the fact that infernal spells might not be as effective against him—even old, powerful stuff like that.

So instead of waiting to see if I had actually bought any real time, I ran my ass off.

When I hit the door to a place called "Hattie's One-Stop Emporium" (because you want your demon store to be properly folksy), I glanced back and saw that Phil was slowly walking toward me like he was trapped in tar, but he was also speeding up the further he made it. So that was just going to be a problem then. Fair enough.

Going on inside, I scanned the shelves for what I needed. Most of the shelves were filled with odd assortments of crap, but finally I found the hallmark of any good truck stop. A dusty case filled with weird and cheaply-made knives. Busting the glass, I pulled out one that had a crudely-realized snake or eagle or something on one end. It should work okay if it didn't break going in. Grimacing at the thought, I ran to the men's bathroom as I heard the front door being pushed open.

I had maybe ten seconds to get this right. Making a cut across my forearm, I sucked in my breath as I used the tip of the blade to slide free a tiny silicone packet holding ten strands of light brown hair.

Cora's hair.

Winding the strands around the knife, I readied my blade over my heart, hoping I had it in the right spot so it would go between my ribs cleanly. While I had never done this ritual before, I felt pretty sure it would work, at least as far as me and Cora were concerned. As for whether I could use it against the homicidal maniac coming to kill me, we would have…

The door began to push open and so I began.

"Hell is a forest deep and dark. Its earth is cold, its trees are stark." Phil was looking at me now, murder in his eyes as he began to reach out slowly.

"One that I love is in Hell's embrace," I pressed the tip of the knife into my chest as I suddenly bolted toward Phil. "so please let me suffer in her place."

As I hit the surprised man, I jammed the knife in as hard as I could, using my impact against Phil's chest to finish driving the point home into my heart. The effect was immediate, and as I felt blackness filling my vision, I wrapped my arms around Phil and held on tightly.

"Let's go for a ride."

****

One second I was sitting in the house of a very strange demon (who had apparently just been stalling until the demonic lynch mob could reach his door for the fresh meat) and then the next I was lying on a dirty bathroom floor. The demon had given me a blanket, but that was gone now, of course. I was back to being naked and cold again, so yay.

Then I saw Teddy's body.

There was a knife sticking out of his chest, and most of the skin on his hands and arms was burned to black. Even with all I had been exposed to lately, it was really hard seeing him like that. And I didn't understand how he had gotten me back this time, as I saw no way he'd have a doll with him. Then it hit me.

I didn't have a doll to bring him back either.

I checked the bathroom quickly for anything he might have left behind—a clue, instructions, something. But there was nothing that I could find. Finally, I went out into what was apparently the truck stop I had seen when we first arrived in Brimley. Looking around for people with no luck, I took some odd souvenir clothing from the shelves, money from the cash register, and keys from a purse I found behind the counter. I didn't like stealing, but I didn't have time to waste. I needed to get back to Teddy's house, and judging from the hundred or so bucks I had gotten from the register and purse, I was going to be driving it. And I had no idea where fucking Brimley even was.

****

Driving through the small town was an eerie experience. It felt like being in the aftermath of a horror movie. I would go for a street or two with no sign of anything being wrong, and then I would find the bodies of a couple of boys or an old man scattered across a sidewalk or driveway. I considered going back to my old body for whatever I might have on me, but I doubted it'd be worth it. I had been traveling light except for the tumerin when I went to get Teddy from the Blind Court, and I really didn't want to run into the thing that killed me again.

So I followed signs until I hit the interstate and then I turned west, going just as fast as possible without running a risk of getting pulled over in a stolen car without a license or anything else. I kept telling myself that Teddy would be fine, but I couldn't know that. I also had the gnawing fear that whatever he had done to bring me back might have messed things up for him to come back via the dolls, but I tried to push the idea aside. I had no real reason to think that. It was just fear talking.

And I had enough to worry about as it was. My latest journey into Hell worried me. I didn't understand what that demon was talking about, and I didn't think I wanted to know. And for all my suspicions that he was just stalling until his demon buddies could come to eat me or poke me with pitchforks or whatever, he had seemed as surprised as I was when they started beating at his door. I would have to ask Teddy about it when there was time.

For now, I pulled up to the house and ran inside, Heckle and Jeckle looking at me with the golem version of surprise and happiness. Not having time for chit chat, I told them to prepare the room for a doll ritual while I went into Teddy's workshop to get his doll.

Even after all these months, I had never been in his workshop before. Entering it now, I found myself slowing to an awed stop at what I was seeing. First of all, it was way bigger than I expected. So much bigger that I didn't understand how exactly it even fit in the house at all. Beyond that, while there was a portion of it that was clearly intended for making the dolls, there were also rows and rows of books neatly shelved and organized.

As I drew closer to them, I saw that many of them looked very old and were written in languages that I either didn't read or had never even seen before. Walking between the bookshelves with amazement, I found myself wondering how much there was that I still didn't know about my Uncle Teddy. That's when I saw a short hallway at the back of his secret occult library. It terminated in a simple wooden door, and I was tempted to go and peek inside, but forced myself back to the task at hand. Every second I wasted was leaving Teddy trapped in Hell longer.

Hurrying back to where he had described he kept our most current dolls, I opened a large wooden chest and found what I was looking for. Carrying his doll back to the ritual room, I found that Heckle and Jeckle had everything ready. Two minutes later, the ritual was complete and the doll was burning.

Except it just kept burning. It didn't disappear, and Teddy didn't come back. I was far from an expert, but in my experience it happened much faster than that. A feeling of panic growing in my chest, I double-checked that all the steps of the ritual had been done properly. When I confirmed the ritual was right, I started to feel a cold feeling crawl up my spine. Maybe he really had messed up his ability to come back via the dolls with whatever he had done to get me back this last time.

I found myself weighing my options, which I knew were few, and I was already checking my phone for the best directions back to Amerson Park when suddenly Teddy was back. Dropping my phone, I ran up to him with a blanket and gave him a quick hug from behind as he stood up. Looking over his shoulder, he gave me a weary grin.

"I told you, I'm not that kind of uncle."

Shoving him in the shoulder, I wiped my eyes with relief. "Shut up."

Teddy headed toward the door to go get dressed when he turned back and looked at me, his face more serious. "Thank you for saving me. Again."

I shrugged and gave him a smile. "It's what we do."

He looked as though he wanted to say more, but finally he nodded and walked out of the room.

My smile faded once he was out of view. Teddy looked okay, but something was still weird. Aside from the abnormal delay in him coming back, he smelled funny. Like sulfur or smoke or something. And when he had looked at me, his eyes were bloodshot. But I didn't understand why that would be. This physical body should never have been in Hell, and besides, what I had seen of Hell didn't smell like fire and brimstone anyway.

More questions for Teddy, but there'd be time for that later, after he had changed and had a chance to rest. For now, things were finally…

There was a knock at the door.

I got Jeckle to stand next to it as I looked out the peephole. It was just a plain-looking older man that I didn't recognize, but that meant very little. I debated waiting until Teddy was back out, but given the golems and the protections on the house, I figured I was safe enough to at least have Jeckle open the door.

"Can I help you?"

The man had looked up as the door had opened, giving me a small smile as he regarded me with cool blue eyes framed by a pair of old-fashioned wire-rimmed glasses. "Hello, Cora." Without waiting for another word, he stepped across the threshold of the door without being invited or allowed in, which I didn't think was even possible. "I'm Christopher Darrow, an old friend of your uncle's. And I think it's time the three of us had a little chat."

Vesper in Hell.

The first thing I noticed, other than the blinding flash of light as the man touched me, was the smell. Or rather how the smell changed. I was slightly familiar with the fairly normal, mundane smells of the men's bathroom at Hattie's One-Stop Emporium. Just a few hours earlier I had actually drug a demon from where they hid in that same bathroom. But this person, whether another demon or a man as he claimed, had done something to me. He had sent me to somewhere that smelled wholly different than the truck stop in Brimley.

The smell was complex and pungent—a mixture of rotten eggs, burning air, and some underlying sweet smell that made my nose run and my eyes water. I blinked and rubbed my eyes, preparing for some further assault by the man and wanting to get my bearings before it came. When my vision cleared enough for me to see, I quickly forgot any ideas of being prepared for anything.

I...I was in Hell. I know that may sound strange, both that Hell exists as a real and physical place and that I could be certain so quickly that I had somehow been transported there, but whether it was due to the darker parts of my creation (if the old man at Wizard's Folly could be believed) or just some innate instinct buried deep within my soul, I knew I was in Hell with a certainty that was both profound and terrifying.It also came as a strange sort of relief. I've been told that I'm some kind of magical Frankenstein monster—an experiment to try and make a creature capable of retaking Hell from a being called "the Hunter". I remembered past versions of myself now, and I knew there was at least some truth in what I was being told. But I also knew I could never help such evil people, even if it would be by fighting another evil. If the Hunter was even evil at all. Amid all my fears and doubts and confusion, the only thing that had seemed constant and true and pure was my bloodlust to kill demons. I didn't know if that was the right answer either, but it certainly felt right as I tore through the crowds that had brought me back to Wizard's Folly. And after that, as I slowly made my way back toward Brimley, I had found myself able to sense whenever one of the monsters was near. I killed dozens at the amusement park before I left, and another five on the way to the town that seemed to be nothing but creatures from Hell.

I wasn't sure how many had stayed behind when we had travelled back for me to see my "father", but after three days of stalking the streets of that town, I had found over four dozen more demons to send back to Hell. And that's how I looked at it when I could think properly--during the periods between the red blind rage and unthinking violence that would always start when I sensed a demon was near. I wasn't killing people, or even killing demons in any meaningful way. I was just sending them back to where they were supposed to be.

Back to Hell.

Still, despite my efforts to reassure myself that I was doing the right thing, the only thing that made sense given my situation, I often found myself wondering if I could trust my mind any more. If I had any humanity left. If I still had a soul.

Those questions went away when my eyes took in the vast landscape of what I would later learn was the chief city of Hell. To call it immense…well, there aren't words to really describe it. I was standing up on a higher part of the city that afforded me a decent view for some distance, and I couldn't begin to see the end of it. There were buildings of all shapes and sizes, and many of them were really very beautiful in a terrible kind of way. There were vast open spaces filled with various shadowy shapes that might have been trees or rock outcroppings of some sort. And in the streets and lanes and paths that writhed through the flesh of that place, there was an endless flood of movement. On the ground, in the sky, burrowing underneath the blasted bits of earth I could make out between structures and inhabitants. The entire scene felt like watching a giant anthill that was perpetually on fire.

Except that was the odd thing. Despite the smell, there was no fire or lava or boiling lakes that I could see. It wasn't even particularly hot. And while I could see very clearly, I didn't see any real sources of light either. Everything just had this faintly luminescent sheen that was both pretty and horrifying at the same time. I had the thought of a shiny black scorpion I had seen on a field trip growing up. It had terrified me, but the part I remembered the most hadn't been its claws or poison-tipped tail. It had been the faint glow its carapace had as it sat there silent, waiting to strike at anything that came too close. It had been beautiful, which somehow made it worse.

That was my first impression of the first and last city of Hell. Its size and grandeur somehow made it more horrible, more dangerous. It looked like a dark leviathan waiting patiently until it was time for its next meal. And maybe that was exactly what it was.

Either way, it confirmed to me that I still was Phil, at least in part, and I still had a soul, such as it might be. Because looking down at the vastness of this small corner of Hell, I felt my soul begin to despair and tremble within me. Then I noticed the naked man who was standing a few feet away waving at me.

I turned toward him, my eyes narrowed. I'd been pretty sure he stabbed himself in the chest when he grabbed me, but I saw no signs of a wound now. More demonic tricks. "You. Why did you bring me here?"

He offered me a sheepish smile. "Yeah, it was a dick move, but necessary. As I told you, I had to get Cora out of

Hell, but if you were still there when she got back, I have a feeling you'd have just murdered her again."

I felt my anger building, but tried to hold it in check. I needed to know more before I killed him. "Maybe. But this is Hell, isn't it?"

"Don't let anyone tell you that you're a stupid homicidal maniac. You're one of the smart ones."

Gritting my teeth, I took a step forward. "Take me back. Now."

He looked less than impressed with my threatening tone, and looking down at my feet, I saw at least one reason why. I was sliding backwards. We were at the edge of a large stone courtyard, and behind the naked man, a massive building of yellow stone reared up into the sky past the edge of my vision. The ground was level and I was trying to walk forward, but for every step I took, I slid back two.

"Yeah, I figured that would be the case." The man was frowning slightly now like he was contemplating a math problem. I wanted to twist his head off. "I don't know much about you, but from what I've heard, you've got a mix of all kinds of magic goodness brewing in you. Including some of the weird juju that the Hunter uses. And this," he pointed back at the yellow building behind him, "is the fifth of the Six Libraries of Hell. Probably the most magically protected places in this realm." Pointing at the tracks I was making as I was pulled away by some magical force, he gave a small smile. "I don't know how long they'll keep the Hunter itself at bay if he ever gets here, but it seems to work a trick on you."

I felt dim panic breaking the surface of my anger. "Please…Get me out of here. I can't stay here."

I was surprised when the man's glib attitude fell away and he looked genuinely sad. "I would if I could, kid. All joking aside, I know you didn't ask for any of this. But I have very limited time and I don't have a way of getting you out right now anyway. I'm working on things that are bigger than you or me. More important."

"Fuck you. I'll kill you." I pushed back against the unseen hand shoving me faster and faster away from the man and the center of the city.

The man shook his head. "You won't, not today. And I have to go. But I'll give you some words of advice before I go. First, stay out of the forest if you can. I don't know how far this magic extends, but there should be an area of infernal Hell you can stay in between the city and the forest. The forest is the Hunter's territory. I know you think you're strong and fast, and you are, but I don't think you'll last long against that thing."

I frowned, feeling a strange sort of pride swelling up at his words. "But I was made to kill it. To be able to beat it."

The naked man shrugged. "Yeah, I guess. But you were also created by evil, selfish fuckups who were desperate. Just because that was their plan doesn't mean it will actually work. Maybe I'm wrong and you can stop it—someday. But I think if you try now you'll be on a suicide mission, except, you know, way worse than just dying."

I was nearly a hundred yards back now and we were having to yell to one another. "Okay. I'll think about what you said. Though I don't know why I should trust you either."

His last words were faint as I rounded a corner and was pulled down a shadowy street toward the city's walls. "You shouldn't! But I'm not as bad as the demons or the Hunter either. To paraphrase *Last of the Mohicans*, 'Stay alive, and I might find you if it isn't overly inconvenient or dangerous for myself or my niece!'"

Very funny, motherfucker.

****

I spent the next…I don't know how time works in this place, so I guess I'll just say "long time" traveling through the city. The beauty and horror that I had witnessed from a distance were only multiplied moving through the bowels of that place. I started moving quicker once I learned to move with the direction I was being pushed, but it was never fast enough. Everywhere I went, people and various creatures would stop and look at me. While none moved to hurt me or stop me, I did hear various whispers, most of which I couldn't understand. Out of those that I could make out, I heard hushed, almost reverent mentions of "Vesper" or "Evening Star".

It made me want to vomit.

In some ways that was the worst part of all this. I constantly had to deal with the unwanted worship, the looks of betrayal and accusatory admonitions when a demon realized I wasn't on their side. They were all whiny, entitled pieces of shit who just assumed I'd be grateful for the chance to have my life and identity ripped away from me so I could go fight some bullshit battle for them in Hell. But at least when I was on Earth, I felt like I was doing some good by killing them. Ridding the world of a little bit of evil. But here? Here they were already where they were supposed to be, and I still had to see and hear them.

The magic that protected the city decided that the place *I* was supposed to be was well outside the city gates, which had opened before I reached them and promptly closed again the moment I was through. A few hundred feet past the wall I felt the resistance at my back fall away, and having no better option, I just kept heading across the rocky plains of the lands beyond.

As I walked, I passed from plains to swamps to a vast orchard filled with burning trees and some kind of flying thing that seemed to scream my name as it swooped and swirled overhead in the darkening sky. Because that was the other thing that changed as I journeyed for what could have been hours or years — everything was growing darker.

I could only see a few feet in front of me by the time I reached the edge of the forest.

My heart began to hammer harder in my chest as I recalled the man's words. I had little fear any more, but what little I had seemed to well up from beneath the hardpan surface of my heart. I didn't know if I should trust the man, but I knew I couldn't trust this place, and in all honesty, I hadn't seen him do anything so far that wasn't defending himself. Deciding to err on the side of caution, I started backing away from the dark woods ahead when I saw something that froze me in place.

It was me.

Part of the reaction I had was due to the shock of seeing my twin staring out at me from the edge of the woods. But a deeper, more visceral part of what happened next was because of something in me…something that recognized that this thing, this double, was the creature they called the Hunter.

Before I could consider, I launched myself forward with all my speed, the only thought thrumming through my mind the heavy drumbeat of kill, kill, kill. I felt the deep cold on my skin as I reached the edge of the forest, and half an instant later I was in the spot where the Hunter had been. Except now he was twenty feet away, giving me a little smile as he waved.

My sudden drive to kill the Hunter made my confidence and certainty temporarily unassailable, but as I chased the Hunter deeper and deeper into the woods, my every attack being easily avoided, I felt that bloodlust cooling as cracks in my resolve began to deepen and widen. He was playing with me. Leading me further into his territory. And I was falling for it.

Pushing my rage and violent urges down, I pivoted quickly back the way I thought I had come. The Hunter was faster than me, but maybe I could get away if I was unpredictable enough. I switched back to an angle that would put me deeper in the woods again, and as I was turning I saw the tree next to me explode into nothingness.

The Hunter was done playing.

I had no idea if I would fare better than that tree had, but I knew I didn't want to find out. So I zigged and zagged, crissed and crossed, trying to confuse the Hunter without overly confusing myself. But it wasn't working. At best I was barely staying ahead of him, at worst he was still just fucking with me. Either way, I needed help or a new plan.

Dodge. Another near miss.

Dart left. Another tree makes a loud cracking sound before just disappearing somehow.

I didn't get tired any more, but I didn't think I could go any faster either. I kept looking for something that might be helpful as the endless stands of trees blurred by, and I almost made the mistake of stopping when I started hearing music playing. I had no way of knowing what that meant, but I was out of options, so I started dodging my way in an irregular pattern toward the sound of that music. It was mixing with the noise from a local waterfall, which made it slightly harder to pinpoint, especially when I was trying to avoid seeming obvious as I searched for it.

After what seemed like an eternity, I saw a small house sitting on the banks of the lake with the small but noisy waterfall at the opposite end. The music was still playing, a sweet and complex tune that sounded like it was being played on a violin or something similar. Trying to prepare for whatever might be inside the house or an attack from behind by the Hunter, I dove toward the front door. It opened easily, and a moment later I was inside a strangely quaint little house.

My first thought was the hobbit houses from the Lord of the Rings movies, even though the only real similarities was the degree of organized clutter and the unrelenting coziness of the place. Its air of welcome was such a stark contrast to the endless barren inhospitality of the forest outside that I gasped as I fell back against the front door. I half-expected it to come thundering down at the Hunter's entry, but there was no sign of the thing that had been stalking me. After several moments without attack, I moved away from the door and further into the house. The music was coming from a warmly-lit living room in the back, the heat of the roaring fireplace a blessing after the cold outside. As I entered the room, I saw the source of the music.

It was a cricket. Or, it wasn't a cricket, it was a monster of sorts, or judging from the corruption I could feel wafting from it, a demon. But it still looked like some kind of giant cricket wearing a bright blue sweater jacket as he sat in a large chair rubbing his legs together. Except instead of making the normal chirruping sound a cricket makes, it was somehow making beautiful music.

Watching it, I wondered for not the first time if I had just gone totally insane. Maybe all this was a fiction of my diseased mind and Marjorie was tearfully watching me from the window of a padded room in an institution somewhere. I felt so lost and alone in that moment, and it wasn't until the cricket demon stood up that I realized he had finally stopped playing. He approached me on his hind legs, but this still only put him at around four feet tall. Looking up, he greeted me with a thin, raspy voice.

"Come sit down, Phillip. I do love having guests, and we have much to talk about."

My Friend Theodore

The first time I met Theodore Westgate, he was a morose-looking young man sitting on a park bench. His eyes were troubled, and you could tell at a glance that he was weighed down by some mundane trouble that life inflicts upon those foolish enough to succumb to such things. He was handsome by most standards, but otherwise appeared unremarkable at first glance.

Unless you looked at his hands.

The smooth precision of his hands as he idly whittled on a piece of wood told more of the truth of him. He was everything I had thought he would be from when I had first passed him outside of a gallery two weeks earlier. Because while that day in the park was the first time I met Teddy, it was not the first time I had ever seen him. And while I never had the Sight the way my sister Radha had it, I've always been able to spot a Dollmaker when the time was right.

It would be easy to chalk up my first passing encounter with something as rare and valuable as Teddy as amazing luck or chance, but I don't believe in coincidence and the odds of someone like me finding a genuine Dollmaker by mere happenstance is absurd. No, I feel the steady, terrifying hand of other influences in such things — what lesser minds might call fate or destiny. But perhaps I am being uncharitable to say lesser minds. Better, and less self-aggrandizing, to say minds that have not seen the wonders and horrors of the world we truly live in.

Because it is a wonderful and horrific place. As a boy growing up outside of Oxford as a poor farmer's son in the late 17th century, I never dreamed of much beyond visiting the city and finding a job and a wife away from the provincial life I had always known. My first experience with the wider world was when I ran away at fifteen, and within six months I was in jail and certain that I would meet a terrible and untimely end.

That wasn't what happened, of course. I was turned loose eventually and found my way into a series of menial jobs around Oxford until I landed a position helping the groundskeeper at the newly-opened Ashmolean Museum on Broad Street. Walking around the interior of that place lit a spark in me that has never been quenched. A thirst for knowledge and the power that it gives you in a world designed to make you feel powerless. I spent the next several years perfecting the art of breaking into local museums and libraries, taking the education that no one would ever give me due to my birth and station.

I was fortunate enough to have been taught basic literacy as a child, but I'd assumed that I would quickly hit the wall of my own limitations when I delved into the high-minded works of true academia. I was wrong. I found myself learning at an alarming pace, and as my palate grew more accustomed to various flavors of knowledge, it also grew more defined.

I found literature to be entertaining, and history was compelling in its own right, but science held a special place in my heart. The unending quest to understand how things truly work seemed like the highest calling one could ask for, and for nearly a decade I dedicated myself to learning the latest theories and principles in physics, chemistry and biology. Ironically, I also became head groundskeeper of the museum during that period of time, but that mattered little other than giving me money for food and more books.

Yet as time passed, I began to feel a growing sense of dissatisfaction with my studies. It wasn't that I was going beyond my capacity to understand. It was that I understood everything all too well. The natural sciences were just another form of religion—a system of slightly educated guesses propped up by the assumed legitimacy of systematic testing and dogmatic adherence to the idea that something that could be replicated was verifiable, and that which was verifiable was *veritas*, or Truth.

But I wasn't finding any real Truth in the study of the natural. So ultimately I turned to the study of the *unnatural*. It was immediately rewarding in ways that my prior studies had not been. Yes, there was the questions of morality, of damnation even, and it wasn't that I didn't believe in my soul. I just didn't know what use it was.

That was my biggest mistake. I wanted to view my soul as a part of me—an appendage like my hand or foot. I'd rather keep it intact, but I could still soldier on without it if need be. Surely I had progressed so far in my knowledge, had amassed such power in the occult in just a few years of study, that myself and my new friends were immune from such frivolous things as Heaven and Hell.

Then I choked to death on a bit of beef.

When I was pulled back from Hell that first time, I cried uncontrollably with relief and terror for nearly three days. My lover at the time, Janet Browning, had surreptitiously had a memoriam doll made for me a few months earlier. While I had to kill her a few years later, I never forgot how she had temporarily saved me from my own hubris and sins.

I say temporarily because it's never really over, is it? You're always running to get more power, more knowledge, to stay one step ahead of the Devil. Or worse still, the Hunter. And one of the greatest assets in that endless race and chase is having a skilled Dollmaker.

****

I am over three hundred years old, and the most important lesson I've ever learned is the dangers of

178

overestimation and underestimation. If you overestimate yourself, you wind up falling prey to your own mistakes and limitations. If you underestimate yourself, you live a small life full of fear and regret. If you overestimate others, you rely on friends that cannot be relied upon. If you underestimate others, you can quickly find yourself outmatched because of arrogant stupidity.

When I was a young man, sitting in a dank cell in Oxford with men twice my age and size, there was an older gentleman everyone called Trilby. I never knew his real name or what he did, but I'll never forget the day two of the inmates decided they didn't like his company anymore. He was too quiet, they said. Stuck up, they said. Needed to be taught a lesson on manners, and they were the ones to do it, or so they thought.

The problem is they meant to pulp up a smallish, middle-aged man who they assumed had little fight in him. Just out of boredom and a general enjoyment of violence, not because they truly hated the man or wanted to see him dead. Trilby, on the other hand, had no interest in them at all. He didn't want to talk to them, but he didn't want to fight them either. And where they came to fight, he came to kill.

I've never forgotten their surprised screams as he gutted them with an odd piece of metal he had found somewhere along the way. And I've never forgotten my own anguished cries when I found myself in Hell that first time, making the same foolish mistake that had gotten those brutes in my cell killed. Thinking I was above it all. Untouchable. That I didn't need anyone or couldn't be beaten.

But being sent to Hell and rescued from it was the last time I needed the lesson repeated. And when I met anyone in the dangerous world I lived in, I always kept in mind the perils of over or underestimating myself or them. That is what has kept me alive this long, and that's how I intend on surviving my latest encounter with my good friend Teddy Westgate.

Because, odd as it may seem, he is my friend. I know he has suffered over the years, and while I would prefer it hadn't been necessary for the needs of myself and the others, it was, as are so many things, a necessary evil. I've always known that Teddy harbors resentment for the life he's had—a life without friends or family or the normal protections most people have to reassure him that he is a "good person", whatever that truly means.

I also know he is very smart and, perhaps even more dangerous, extremely clever. He has made a point of learning more occult knowledge than is necessary for his work, and he has also made a point of hiding how much he knows. I provided him with most of the materials myself, explaining to him that I knew he was curious about these things and I was happy to furnish him with materials that furthered his ability as a Dollmaker.

Of course, I made sure I gave him materials that included other topics as well. I knew his interests went beyond just becoming more proficient at making memoriam dolls, and my hope has always been that he would see my providing broader ranged occult knowledge as an acknowledgment and respect for that. I also hoped that it would satiate the growing hunger for knowledge I recognized in him and give him a preoccupation beyond hating what his life had become.

Yet I also recognized the dangers of giving a man like Teddy too much knowledge. So most of the books I gave him were...altered to a degree. It took a great deal of effort and expense, but for years I've been feeding him books that were almost exact replicas of ancient texts and arcane rituals. Almost exact because, while some of it would be exactly correct— namely anything related to dollmaking or unrelated matters that he could easily test or verify on his own—other parts, parts that could lead down the paths of significant power and understanding, were altered enough in subtle ways that he would be prevented from progressing too far. My thought was that the solution was mutually beneficial in the end — Teddy had a satisfying hobby where he felt he was gaining the power needed to eventually secure his emancipation, and I had less headaches worrying he might be amassing real power that would make him more difficult to control.

Of course, there are no guarantees in anything. He could have figured out that I was tricking him, but even if that were the case, it was highly unlikely he would have the ability to pose a real threat to me with whatever genuine knowledge he may have acquired over the years. Still, I admit to feeling some worry as the door opened and I saw his troublesome niece looking at me warily. When I introduced myself and walked in, I felt considerable relief that I felt no magical resistance to my entry. When the girl tried to sic her pet golems on me, my ability to bind them and honestly threaten their destruction until she called them off emboldened me further.

Things were as I had left them, as they should be. And when Teddy came out in a robe, he gave me a warm hug and told Cora to sit down, to quit glaring at his old friend. My good friend Theodore still understood the dynamics of his relationship with me despite his conflicts with the others. Good. Very good. Things were off to a nice start, and if it continued going this way, I might only have to kill the girl. For good this time. I didn't want to break Teddy, but I did have to teach him not to bite.

But first, I needed to see the lay of the land. Break the ice, talk things out, and see what my options really were. I think I'll start out with some jokes. Teddy always seemed to like that.

Uncle Teddy and Cora: The Dollhouse

"So one day Jim Morrison of *The Doors* died in Paris, and as you'd imagine all of his family and friends were heart-broken, especially his wife."

"Um, I don't think Jim Morrison was married when he died."

Uncle Teddy gave me a withering look of disapproval. "He's telling a joke, Cora. Don't be rude." I glared back at him as I sunk further into my chair with folded arms. I didn't like the direction this was heading *at all*. First this asshole shows up, comes in like he owns the place (past magic wards that I thought would have kept him out), and then when I tell Heckle and Jeckle to stop him, he somehow freezes them in place and tells me he'll kill them if I don't call them off.

The worst part was, I could tell he wasn't bluffing. He could do magic in here, and given the fact that he was the person that recruited Teddy into the life of a Dollmaker all those years ago, I thought it was fair to say he wasn't a good guy. I held out some dim hope that Teddy would come out and fix things with some sinister threat or clever plan, but instead, he had actually seemed happy to see Darrow. They had slapped backs and laughed, Teddy had told the golems to bring us in some drinks and snacks, and now we were apparently sitting down to chit-chat and tell jokes with one of the most dangerous occultists still alive in the world. I kept hoping Teddy was just buying us time until he figured things out, but that hope was fading fast, and I honestly couldn't tell if my uncle was terrified of the man and just trying to placate him by being pleasant, or worse, he was actually friends with this guy.

With the way he was laughing it up and scolding me

when I dared correct the evil fuck, my fear and anger were racing each other for my tongue. I was trying to slow them down, but it was hard, and I knew it was only a matter of time before I was doing more than interrupting his stupid joke.

Darrow cleared his throat as he gave me a dry smile. "As I was saying. So we come to Jim Morrison's wake, and everyone is there of course. The band is in line to view his body, with the keyboardist at the back. Suddenly, someone pokes him from behind. When he turns around, he sees that it's God."

Teddy gave a small chuckle and nod as he listened. I was paying attention, as I couldn't say for sure that none of this was important, but I felt my impatience growing. If I could just reach my room, I had a gun and…

"God smiles at the keyboardist and says, 'Hey, man. Sorry for your loss. Jim was a good guy. But given how you just lost your lead singer and all…well, things aren't looking too bright for the band. What do you say about signing up with me? I've got a lot of contacts, as you might imagine, and I guarantee you'll be happier than you ever were with whoever is managing you now."

"The keyboardist is kind of shocked by the offer, and he tells God that now isn't the time or the place for such talk. God looks disappointed but seems to understand."

"The next day, the keyboardist is sitting in the church during Jim's funeral. Suddenly, he realizes that God is sitting next to him with a knowing smile. 'Hey, just wanted to check in with you. I have the contract right here. Higher album percentages, two guaranteed solo albums with backend on any concerts or merch. What do you say?"

"Again, the keyboardist refuses to talk about closing any deal. 'Later', he whispers, trying to not be overheard by the rest of the band and poor Jim's wife. Again, God seems disappointed and leaves."

"Now we're at the graveside. Well-wishers and fans are coming by to give their condolences, and the keyboardist sees with some dread that God is in the line and approaching him. Before God can even speak, the keyboardist finally relents— "Fine, fine, I'll sign with you, okay?"

"God smiles broadly and gives him a hug. "That's wonderful!" With that, the Almighty pulls out a large straight razor and slashes Jim Morrison's wife open from top to bottom before leaving the graveyard with a small wave."

Teddy burst out laughing as I shook my head. "Jesus."

Darrow looked over at me with a mockingly dour look. "What? Didn't get it, my dear?"

I rolled my eyes. "Oh, I got it. When God closes a Door, he opens a widow, right?"

The man smiled thinly and nodded. "Just don't appreciate gallows humor I suppose. Ah well, more's the…"

I stood up, my fists clenched at my sides. I was trying to give Teddy time to do whatever it was he was going to do, if anything, but I was tired of waiting. Time to tip this douche over a little and see what scuttled out. Some information, a reaction, a mistake, something.

"No, what I don't appreciate is you walking in like you own the fucking place," I turned and shot Teddy a look, "through magical wards or shields or whatever that are supposed to keep anyone from coming in or doing magic unless one of us okays it. I know *I* didn't okay it. Did you, Teddy?"

Teddy looked at me with wide eyes, his expression both fearful and sheepish. "Cora…I…um…"

Darrow was chuckling again now, but it had lost any pretense of friendliness or warmth. It was a cold, nasty sound that made me suppress a shudder as he stood up and turned to face me. "Don't blame poor Teddy. His wards work just fine. It's just…well, who do you think put the wards up for him in the first place, girl?" His eyes twinkled with dark merriment as he took a step toward me. "And who do you think you are to speak to me like this?"

Uncle Teddy stood up hesitantly, his voice trembling slightly. "Christopher, she's just a girl. She doesn't understand everything, and she's been through quite a lot. We both have. Have mercy on her."

I felt my stomach turn to ice. Teddy really was scared of this man. I had never seen Teddy afraid like this, and it was terrifying. Swallowing thickly, I nodded. "He's right. I'm just upset. I'm sorry I was rude." Sitting back down, I kept my eyes lowered. "I hope you accept my apology."

Out of my peripheral vision I saw Darrow move back to his chair. When he spoke, his tone was slightly warmer. "Good, good. I want my reunion with my friend Teddy to be a happy one. We have much to talk about. You've been very busy." I looked up and saw Darrow had turned his focus back to Teddy now that I had been put in my place. My mind racing, I tried to come up with some way out of this for us, but for now I didn't know enough to know what might work. For all I knew, Darrow could kill us both with a thought. Or worse.

"Yes, I knew you'd hear about some of that." Teddy smiled weakly. "But I assure you, it was all self-defense and necessary."

Darrow let out another small laugh. "Self-defense, eh? The Blind Court, possibly. The caretakers of *Die Hungrige Klinge*? From what I've heard, you sought them out and slaughtered them. But I don't really care, so we'll call that a wash. But members of my own Circle? Friends and confidants that I've known for decades? For centuries? That's a different matter entirely. They trusted you, Teddy. I trusted you."

Teddy frowned slightly. "Didn't you always tell me that this work you do requires strength of will and mind? Didn't I do you a favor by getting rid of members that were stupid enough to fall for my tricks?"

Darrow broke into what seemed like a genuine grin. "Teddy, Teddy. You're right, of course. There wasn't one in that whole bunch worth as much as you. Most of them would have proven to be more of a liability than an asset in the times that are coming." His grin began to falter as he went on. "That being said, times are coming. Plans are in motion. Delicate plans that you are disrupting with your chaos."

When Teddy stayed silent, Darrow continued. "Or do you think I don't know that you sent the Evening Star to Hell?" He frowned sourly. "That was always Frank's pet project, not mine, and frankly I think he stands little chance against the Hunter, but that didn't mean he wasn't potentially useful as we prepare for the Breach. All you've done is sent him to be slaughtered."

Uncle Teddy went to speak but Darrow waved him quiet again. "I'm not finished. I have given you everything all these many years...kept you safe and protected. My plan was to ensure that you survived the coming change and had a place with me and mine. That may still come to pass, but...well, there's no easy way to say this." He turned to stare at me, his stony gaze boring through me as he continued to talk to Teddy. "This girl, this niece of yours, she's proven to be a bad influence. I don't know if she's some reminder of your former life, someone you've been trying to impress, or just a general troublemaker, but she has to go. Permanently."

Teddy let out a long, sad sigh like a balloon losing the last of its air. His voice small and hollow, he whispered, "Go ahead then. Get it over with."

I had time to feel a rush of pain and sadness that Teddy

didn't even try to defend me before Darrow was standing again. He made several complex gestures with his hands as he stepped forward, his voice sonorous with dark mumblings that seemed to burn the air as he spoke. I had a final thought that I hoped Teddy would be okay and then Darrow slammed his hands together with a finality that sounded like the cracking of the world.

But nothing happened.

Behind him, Teddy was smirking. "What's the matter, Christopher? Can't get it up?"

Darrow whirled on him. "What did you do?"

Teddy gestured to the empty chair. "Sit down and I'll tell you."

The other man took a threatening step toward my uncle. "You'll tell me no…" Then he was yanked off his feet and flung into the chair. The chair itself almost tipped over, but was somehow robbed of its backwards momentum and righted at the last moment. Darrow was still sitting in the chair like a pinned bug, his eyes wide and filled with a combination of fear and hate as he glared at Teddy.

My uncle didn't seem concerned. "I think we're done with the portion of this encounter where I let you act like a patronizing ass who's in control of things. As you are starting to figure out, you are in control of very little at this point."

Darrow looked like he was trying to swallow a particularly unsavory piece of gristle as he cleared his throat and tried to regain his composure. It was disquieting to see how quickly he was able to do so. Within seconds he was smiling a cold smile, and when he spoke, his tone was measured and careful.

"Do you mind telling me how you accomplished all this?"

Teddy's eyes glittered as he leaned forward in his chair. He looked at Darrow for several seconds before turning to me. "See, Cora, this is the point where he expects the villains, namely us, to explain the inner workings of their plan. Because rest assured, Christopher sees us as the villains in this simply because we are obstacles to what he wants. He wants to kill you because you're a bad influence on me. And he wants to see if I can be brought in line. If I'll stay loyal after watching you get sent to Hell for a final time."

"I'm right here, Teddy. Talk to me." Darrow's tone was harsher now, and it looked as though his calm demeanor was beginning to crack.

Ignoring him, Teddy continued. "The problem, my dear niece, is that Christopher is very smart. Maybe not smarter than you, but certainly smarter than me. And he's proud of that intelligence, particularly when it comes to matters such as this, where intellect and will are of such great importance. He's so proud, in fact, that he thinks he can't be beaten. He's always three steps ahead of everyone else, you see."

I eyed Darrow warily. "So he's really powerless here? You've really got him for sure?"

Teddy smiled as he sat back in his chair. "Well, it would be a bit of ironic hubris for me to say he's beaten with 100% certainty after just going into Christopher's pride being his downfall, but just between you and me…," He cupped his hand theatrically as he did a loud stage whisper in my direction. "Yeah, he's super duper fucked."

I felt relief flowing through me as though a new wellspring had been tapped in my chest. Quick behind it was mild irritation. "Asshole. You could have let me in on the joke. I've been freaking out over here."

Teddy was still smiling as he nodded, but his eyes were harder and more distant now. "I understand, and I hated it.

But I didn't want to risk Christopher catching on until I was ready. Not because it would have made much of a difference in what happens to him, but because it makes a difference to me." He swung his gaze back to Darrow, and for the first time, I saw open fear on the other man's face. "You stole so much from me. You all did. Not to mention all the terrible shit you've done to other people and the things you still have planned. You're owed a lot of suffering, and I find it always hurts worse when its unexpected."

Darrow's lower lip trembled with some foul mixture of rage, despair, and terror. *"How are you doing this?"*

Uncle Teddy cocked a thumb at Darrow as he looked at me with a raised eyebrow. "Do you believe this guy? He's still more concerned about how I did it than what's going to happen to him. He still thinks he can win this, particularly since he's been feeding me bad information for so long." I saw Darrow flinch at that. Teddy noticed it too and let out a little chuckle. "You want to know how smart my buddy Chris is? He's so smart, so sly and careful, he had incorrect duplicates of various arcane texts created just so he could give them to me. Teach me the wrong way of doing spells and rituals that didn't relate to my role as a pet Dollmaker." He raised his hand. "And it worked for years. A lot of that was my fault, but in my defense, they were masterfully done. The books looked authentic, and he made sure that enough of the information was right, enough of the things in the books would kinda sorta work, that I would think I was learning the real deal, with any problems due to my mistakes rather than flaws in the texts."

He turned and regarded Darrow again, his expression stony. "But I knew how smart Chris was. He'd made sure I knew over the years. So I decided to get some of my own super-rare occult texts from other sources. I just...well, I just had a hunch." He smiled thinly. "And what do you know? I knew enough to be able to spot the differences and tell which one was wrong. After that, I'd still thank Mr. Darrow for the light reading, but I knew not to trust anything in the books that I didn't independently verify. Time-consuming work, but then again, they made sure I had plenty of time by myself for recreational reading."

I wanted to ask more questions, but I decided to let Teddy talk it out. For one thing, this was a big moment for him—finally getting revenge on the person that brought him into this life. For another, my uncle was kind of terrifying at the moment. I had seen him angry and ruthless before, of course, but this was somehow different. There was a kind of cold rage threaded through his words and gestures that I had only seen glimpses of before now. It was an anger bred from loss and guilt and shame, and it needed to be fed with the suffering of those that wronged him. Judging from what I was seeing, it was very hungry, and I knew it was best to just stay quiet for now.

Darrow wasn't as smart.

"Congratulations, Teddy. You finally realized you were a fool. It took you long enough. Why don't you get this all over with? You're beginning to bore me." Darrow's tone was condescending, but I could still see the fear in his eyes. He was trying to goad Teddy into killing him, but he was also terrified of the prospect. Still, if he was so scared of going to Hell, why…

"…do you want to go to Hell all of a sudden? You've always been terrified of going before, even with my dolls to guarantee a way back, and it's reasonable for you to assume I'd do a tainted doll ritual as soon as you were dead to insure memoriam dolls were no longer an option for you. So what's different now…" Teddy's mind was on the same track mine was, but I saw he already had the answer. "Unless you either have another way back or you've decided to finally sack up and stay in Hell for a bit."

Now I did speak up. "Why would he want to stay in Hell? Isn't he afraid of the Hunter getting him?"

Teddy nodded. "Oh yeah, I'm sure he is. But Christopher is a master occultist. I bet he knows that there are ways you can influence where you land in Hell. And not all of Hell is forest, is it, Chris?"

The man's eyes bulged. "You went to the City?"

Teddy gave him a wide smile, his eyes dangerous. "Oh yes. Nice place. Been several times now. I even got a local library card."

Darrow's eyes closed tightly as he began trembling with what I hoped was impotent rage. "You went to the Libraries. Of course. I still don't see how…but that's the only thing that makes sense." He opened his eyes again, his gaze clear and unwavering. "Teddy, you're right. You've beaten me. And yes, I was going to finally go to the Libraries and try to learn all I could before the Breach. But I wanted you to be on my side for all of that. You were useful before as a Dollmaker, but I see now how much I've underestimated you. Wronged you." He nodded toward me. "I also see that young Cora is an asset. It was foolish to threaten her." Licking his lips, he gave Teddy a nervous smile. "But none of that changes what's coming. The Breach will occur soon, and if the Hunter still exists when that happens, we are all doomed. Let's work together. I feel sure we can win if we do."

Teddy seemed deep in thought as he stood up. "It's an interesting proposition. I'll be right back." He was headed out of the parlor when I called to him.

"What the fuck? You leaving me alone with the evil wizard guy?"

Teddy rolled his eyes. "Just for a minute. I have to get something before I forget."

I half-expected him to come back in with a weapon of some kind, but instead he was carrying what looked like a large doll's head. Even from a distance I could tell it resembled Darrow, even if it was twice the size of his actual head. When Teddy was back in the man's field of vision, Darrow let out a wail.

"Oh, good. So you have some idea of what this is. That cuts down on unnecessary exposition then." He opened the head along a hidden vertical seam and fitted it down on Darrow's shoulders. I had time to see four long needles at different points along the interior before he closed the doll head around Darrow's own with a slightly meaty-sounding snap. The man's wail turned into a screech that reminded me of a teakettle, boiling on for several seconds before fading away with a wetly terrible final gasp.

Teddy looked up at me, his expression more relaxed. "Well good. That's done then."

Standing up, I started pacing. So much had happened in the last half hour that I felt like I was on the verge of having a stroke. "What the fuck? What the fuck with all of this? What is that thing? Didn't you just kill him and give him what he wants?"

Laughing a little, Teddy raised his hands. "Whoa, whoa. Slow your roll. I guess some explanation is in order."

Glaring at him, I tried to make myself stop walking the room, momentarily contenting myself with fidgeting as I leaned against the wall. "Um yeah. As I said, 'what the fuck'."

Teddy nodded. "Fair enough. Okay, so like I said, I've known for some time that Darrow was trying to feed my desire to learn more magic with doctored texts. He really did do a good job on them, but I still learned enough that I started picking up on the flaws and cross-checking anything he gave me whenever possible. Yet, for all my years of study, I knew a fraction of what someone like Milly knew, much less one of the really old, powerful Circle leaders like Darrow. One reason for this is because they don't like to share."

"But there's one area that it's easier to learn about because, ironically enough, most black magicians don't want to dwell on it more than necessary. That was knowledge of Hell itself."

****

Every true practitioner of black magic knows where that road leads, and while they'll spend a great deal of time, money, and effort learning how to avoid or limit any time in Hell, they get very squeamish when it comes to the details of the place itself.

How it works. Its history and nature. Even obviously useful things like how magic works there or the Realm's geography.

I first recognized the willful blindness these assholes seem to share a few years ago, and once I did, I saw a small crack I might fit through. I started directing more of my secret efforts to gain occult knowledge toward information on Hell itself, and while it was scarce, it was out there. The stuff didn't exactly read like a travel guide, and much of it was very odd and obscure, but over time I developed quite a bit of knowledge of the place.

For instance, I think I mentioned before that Hell didn't start when Lucifer and his angels fell there. It already existed, although it was much different. More importantly though, it was already occupied. The things that were there…well, they were extremely powerful and very old even back then. There was some fighting when the angels arrived, but for the most part they seemed to just…leave. No one is sure where they went other than some oblique references I've found that they are still waiting "Outside". Outside of what, I'm not sure. But that's less important for our current lesson on our favorite vacation getaway.

I said for the *most part* they left. There was one that stayed behind and fought to keep Hell. It was apparently the least of these beings, and it still destroyed over half of the forces Lucifer had at his disposal. And when I say destroyed, that's exactly what I mean.

There's no death in Hell. Not really. If you die, where else would you go anyway? But the Hunter sends people and demons somewhere, right? I've heard his power called "paracausal magic" — magic that is distinct from Infernal or terrestrial magic because it is not bound by the same rules of a particular Realm or our reality. I think this being, this remnant of the old, first Hell, might have had a weaker, less refined version of the same thing. Either way, it took all of Lucifer's armies to kill it, and even now its body lies at the furthest edge of Hell.

The City, as Christopher called it, is the capital of Hell. It goes by many names, but the City works well enough. It was built initially by Lucifer as a fortification near that leviathan's corpse — just in case it was only *mostly dead* and ever woke again. It never has, and the City has continued to grow over time. And not just the City.

Have you ever wondered why the Hunter hasn't fully taken over Hell after all this time? He's had hundreds of years, right? Part of it is because Hell truly is vast. The other part is because it keeps getting vastier.

Hell never stops growing. For every mile the Hunter takes, another mile (or maybe two) grow up between him and the edge of Hell. It's like stretching demonic taffy that never gets thinner or breaks. In theory, that sounds like it might be a good thing. The Hunter is super shitty, and if old Infernal Hell is a slightly less shitty alternative, isn't it good to keep at least some of it out of the Hunter's grasp? Well, yes, but the growing is still a big issue. Because of the Breach.

****

"Hang on a minute."

Teddy raised an eyebrow. "Question?"

We were still in the parlor, Darrow's mask slowly dripping blood out of the bottom as me and Teddy had story time. It was disconcerting, but I had faith that Teddy knew what he was doing. But all this new information? "Why didn't you tell me more of this before?"

Teddy sighed. "I was getting to that, but I can jump to that part I guess. I had never actually been to Hell before the time I committed suicide and you brought me back. As you know, part of my reason for going was to get hair from the Hunter for our little dinner party. The other reason was to visit the Libraries of Hell."

****

There are Six Libraries of Hell, or there were, and they contain the collective knowledge of Hell on many subjects, including various forms of magic. They are, as you might guess, immense, but they have a couple of unique features as well. First, they have magic protecting them that makes it difficult for the Hunter, or anything tainted by paracausal magic, to get near them. That is another reason the Hunter's progress, while steady, has been slower as he gets closer to the City, as all the Libraries reside there. Second, while time is very different in Hell than it is here, it is almost nonexistent in the Libraries.

During the few days I was dead before you brought me back the first time, I spent what would have likely felt like months or years in Hell. Except I spent over half that time in the Libraries, so those months or years became centuries. I had tried to prepare myself for what that would be like—the loneliness, the strangeness of it all—and there are certain spells that can help cushion the negative effects of that much time alone and help you retain more, but they can only help so much and my knowledge and skills were pretty limited. I won't dwell on the details, but the short version is it was very hard, but I got through it, left the Library and had my…disagreement with the demon, got the Hunter's hair, and you brought me back.

The second time I went to Hell was during the big party, and my primary focus then was to find you and stick together until our dolls pulled us back, so no trips to the lieberry. The third time was when I died in Brimley. Back to the Libraries I went. That trip was much more productive because I knew a lot more and had a much better idea of how the Libraries actually work.

Each of the Libraries are different in many ways, but they do share some commonalities. First, you are always alone in them. That's not to say there aren't various other beings in the Libraries when you are, but they are usually just shadowy glimpses now and then. It's like everyone is on their own frequency. It makes things lonelier, but it does make it much safer and easier to focus on learning what you came for.

Second, the Libraries are much bigger on the inside than they are on the outside. Like way bigger. It's a similar magic to what the Blind Court used in their blood tesseract, though it is much more refined and efficient. It took some time on that first trip, but I managed to learn a janky version of how it worked before you brought me back. More on that later.

Third, the term "library" is kind of stretched to its limits when you're talking about the Libraries of Hell. Yes, there are endless mazes of books, scrolls, charts, you name it. But there are many other things as well. They are all designed to store and potentially impart knowledge of one sort or another, but the harder stuff…the more valuable stuff…well, it can be tricky and more dangerous to get.

Finally, what I suspected on my first trip and confirmed on my second, is that the most powerful magic and information is split up between the Libraries. You might have a spell or an old history of some important event divided between several or all of the Libraries, meaning you have to visit them all and search out the information. That's another reason I had to work fast when I went there from Brimley.

On that second trip, I spent a great deal of time at the second and third libraries. Even with magical help and prior experience, I can only find things so fast and remember so much, so my knowledge is very patchy and incomplete. I have learned several things that will help us greatly I think, but I still have much more I need to learn.

****

"Hold up." I waved my hand to stop Teddy. "So you're saying we're still not done with the Libraries? We have to go back to Hell again?"

Teddy frowned slightly. "Well, yes. There are several threads I'm following that might lead to answers for how we can stop the Breach or the Hunter, but I don't know yet. And while you don't have to go with me, I won't deny having your help would be great."

My heart was hammering in my chest at the thought of going back there, even if it was to a library in the non-Huntery part of Hell. I pointed to Darrow. "But you've got enough magic to beat his ass now. No chance of making do with that?" I knew the answer as I said it, but I had to try.

Teddy grinned at me. "I've got enough magic and understanding of Christopher to *trick* his ass so that he beats himself. I don't know that I would win any kind of wizard duel or whatever Harry Potter gobbledygook you might be imagining." He ignored my dark look and went on. "The reason we beat him wasn't because I'm stronger than him. It's because he walked into a trap. As I said, when I went into the first Library, I made it a point to figure out a method of replicating the way the Library worked. A magical tesseract — a pocket dimension where I set all the rules."

"Our house...it isn't the real house. It took weeks after the party, but I magically recreated our house down to the smallest detail and then sat it down on top of the real thing. Anyone who passes through a door or window or any boundary of this place is actually stepping from the real world to our version of the house, though they'd never know the difference unless they were very skilled in magic and looked very closely. The problem for them is, they have to be inside to see it at all, and by that point they are already trapped."

I raised an eyebrow. "Okay. So I get letting Darrow think he was in control when he first got here, stopping the golems, being a dick, all that. But are you telling me you have a bunch of demons chained up somewhere to power all this?"

Teddy stood up beaming. "That's the best part. Like I said, the version that I'm using is a janky version of the Libraries' magical tesseract spell. But it is still way more efficient than the blood tesseract the Blind Court was using. I've ran it so far on just a little bit of my own lifeforce now and then. Maybe took of a few months or a couple of years my natural lifespan at most."

Now I stood up. "Teddy, no. We have to figure out another way..."

He raised a finger. "I already have." He had reached Darrow's body and gave the giant doll head a large tap. "This contraption is very interesting. After being applied for a few minutes, it shunts a person's soul from the brain, which is usually the physical tethering point for one's spirit, to...well, the torso? I'm not sure if it's the heart, the colon, or what exactly, but it pushes it down there and preserves the body indefinitely."

I wasn't sure I would like the answer, but I asked anyway. "Preserves it how and for what?"

Teddy's grin got wider as he thumbed a latch on the bottom of the doll's head. There was a large metallic clang like a bear trap being sprung, and then the doll's head rolled off and onto the floor, carrying Darrow's head with it. I stepped back with a small yelp as Teddy chuckled darkly.

"Darrow doesn't get to die. I can't risk him roaming around Hell or coming back here, and he deserves worse than that. And he's also too dangerous to keep as a prisoner, even in the little dollhouse that I've made for us. But it's his knowledge and intelligence that makes him so deadly. So the doll head's job was to first give him a magical lobotomy before going to work shoving his dirty soul down his throat and into his pancreas or whatever. Because, at least when it comes to humans, all magical power is stored and channeled through the soul. And even though Christopher's soul is no doubt a toxic waste dump, it still has a lot of power."

I nodded, giving Teddy a small smile. "Enough power to be a battery for our new house?"

"Exactly!" He looked pleased for a moment before his eyes fell to the doll's head on the floor. "That thing just keeps leaking blood. The neck stump is sealed properly, but Chris' stupid head has really ruined this rug. Oh well." Suddenly the doll head was gone and the blood-soaked rug was clean. "That's better."

I was feeling much better about things overall, even with the looming dangers of what was coming and what we still had to do. And I still had a lot of questions, but one stood out to me as the most important.

"So what exactly is the Breach?"

Teddy's expression darkened, and after a moment's consideration, he grabbed a piece of burned wood from the fireplace and crouched down. He drew a large circle of ash on the floor and then a smaller one inside it. Looking up at me, he said, "This is a rough approximation of an old cosmological drawing I saw one time from a French occultist named Trudeau or something. I don't know if it's right or not, but it will work for our purposes."

Pointing his stick at the smaller inner circle, he said. "This is us. Our universe, and all the alternate versions of this universe that might exist if you believe that sort of thing." He pointed to the larger outer circle. "These are the Realms. There are supposedly Seven Realms, and one of them is Hell." He looked troubled as he waved his stick beyond the circles. "Outside of that…well, no one knows, though some think that's where the first occupants of Hell went to."

Moving back to the center circle, he went on. "The more pressing point is this. Hell is not only always growing, it's growing *inward*. Meaning it is getting closer and closer to our reality. Now normally it might just reach that boundary and stop…like soap bubbles pressing up against each other. The problem is the edge of Hell has the corpse of some cosmic horror sitting there like a battering ram. A battering ram that is likely still imbued with significant amounts of reality-breaking paracausal magic. Maybe enough to breach the border of our universe and send Hell spilling in." Standing back up, his face was serious. "So that's the Breach. And that's why we have to stop it."

"Fuck."

He nodded. "Yes. Fuck." There was a moment of dour silence between us before his face brightened. "But cheer up. We're on the right track I think. All we have to…"

"Why did you smell weird when you came back today?"

Teddy gave me a mock offended look. "What did I smell like?"

"Um, smoke and brimstone. I figured that must just be what non-Huntery Hell smells like, but why did you smell *at all*? Don't you get a new body when you come back? One that's never been in Hell at all?"

He nodded. "Normally, yes. But when I went the first time, I had to have a way back *with* the Hunter's hair. So before I killed myself, I spent months figuring out not only how to steer where I landed in Hell, but also how to give myself a new physical body there instead of when I got pulled back by the doll. It's more dangerous, and as you saw, it led to me popping back with injuries from that stupid demon I double-crossed, but it does let you physically bring stuff back with you, which can be very useful."

His eyes took on a devilish glint as he continued. "As for the smell, normal Hell doesn't really smell like much of anything, or at least not uniformly. It's not like an old cartoon full of fire and brimstone, at least not from what I've seen. No, the smell came from the first three Libraries. When I was finished this time, I burned all three of them down."

My eyes widened. "You *burned them down*? How? Aren't they super magically protected?"

He smiled. "They are. Super-duper even. But there are always cracks to get through, and I've had a lot of time to figure out where they are."

Shaking my head slowly, I sat back down. "But all that knowledge. There's more there that could help us, right? Now it's just gone?"

Teddy came and knelt beside me, his eyes locked on

mine. "More that could help our enemies too. They're terrified of Hell, which is why most of them, even Darrow, haven't tried to use the Libraries before. But between the Hunter and us, they're getting more desperate, more dangerous. They can't be allowed to learn some of the things I've learned." He put his hand on mine and gave it a squeeze. "And don't fall into the trap of assuming knowledge is always a good thing. That's their way of thinking. They think that understanding more, becoming more powerful, justifies everything they do. I'm learning what I need to stop them and keep us safe, that's all. And if you decide to come with me, you have to promise to do the same. It's a dangerous, slippery road we're walking, and you know what they say about the road to Hell."

"It's super shitty." I squeezed his hand back and smiled. "I promise. And of course I'm coming with you when you go back."

He stood up, but not before I saw the relief on his face. "That means a lot to me, Cora. And if it's any consolation, it'll be a bit before we go back anyway. We need time to rest and recuperate, or as you might say 'chillax', and..."

"I would never say 'chillax'. No one says 'chillax'."

He sniffed dismissively as he went on, "and we have several projects to complete before we're ready to go back. I think it might be a bit rougher going next time. You ready to eat something? I'm fucking starving."

I swallowed, trying to keep my voice light. "Oh? Rougher? Why's that?"

Teddy shrugged as he headed toward the kitchen. "Well, the things that run the City? I think when I burned down half of their most valuable resource, I kinda pissed them off." He paused and glanced back at me. "I don't know about you, but I'm feeling compelled to eat empanadas."

Lowering my face into my hands, I nodded bleakly.

"Goddamnit.   Yes, empanadas do sound really good right now."

www.ingramcontent.com/pod-product-compliance
Lightning Source LLC
Chambersburg PA
CBHW030919060726
47591CB00005B/1605

9 781797 056357